THE
VANISHING
FOOTPRINTS

Adventures
of the Northwoods

1. *The Disappearing Stranger*
2. *The Hidden Message*
3. *The Creeping Shadows*
4. *The Vanishing Footprints*

THE VANISHING FOOTPRINTS

Lois Walfrid Johnson

BETHANY HOUSE PUBLISHERS
MINNEAPOLIS, MINNESOTA 55438

Andrew Anderson number 3, Big Gust Anderson, Walfrid Johnson, Reverend Pickle, Charles Saunders, Peter Schyttner, and Oscar Thorssen lived in the Grantsburg/Trade Lake area of northwest Wisconsin in the early 1900s. All other characters are fictitious. Any resemblance to persons living or dead is coincidental.

Cover illustration by Andrea Jorgenson.

Published by Bethany House Publishers
A Ministry of Bethany Fellowship, Inc.
6820 Auto Club Road, Minneapolis, Minnesota 55438

Printed in the United States of America

Library of Congress Cataloging-in-Publication Data

Johnson, Lois Walfrid.
    The vanishing footprints / Lois W. Johnson.
        p.   cm. — (The Adventures of the northwoods ; bk. 4)
    Summary: Kate, Anders, and Erik try to solve the mystery of the stolen creamery checks.

    [1. Swedish Americans—Fiction.   2. Mystery and detective stories. 3. Christian life—Fiction.]
I. Title. II. Series: Johnson, Lois Walfrid. Adventures of the northwoods ; bk. 4.
PZ7.J63255Van   1991
[Fic]—dc20   91–15042
ISBN 1–55661–103–X   CIP
                                                                    AC

To Daryl, Gail, and Jessica,

because you've discovered
the gift of reading
together.

LOIS WALFRID JOHNSON is a well-known author among Christian readers. In 1989 she won a Gold Medallion award for her series *Let's-Talk-About-It Stories For Kids*, which includes the books *Secrets of the Best Choice* and *You're Worth More Than You Think!* Her pre-teen devotionals *You're My Best Friend, Lord* and *Just a Minute, Lord* have been bestsellers for several years. She and her husband, Roy, have three children and live in rural Wisconsin.

CONTENTS

1. Danger Ahead! 9
2. Trouble at Trade Lake 16
3. Going Fishing 23
4. Discovery! 30
5. Nighttime Search 37
6. Letter From Sweden 44
7. Accident! 51
8. Two Promises 58
9. The Mysterious Message 64
10. The Vanishing Footprints 72
11. Sounds From the Darkness 77
12. The Secret Room 85
13. More Bad News 91
14. The Butter Tub Disaster 97
15. Sunday Deadline 105
16. Thin Ice! 111
17. Lars's Question 118
18. The Lost Fiddle 123
19. Another Warning 129
20. Snatched From the Fire............................135
21. Ride Into Fear 141
22. Bone-Chilling Surprises 149
Acknowledgments 157

1

Danger Ahead!

*W*hen Katherine O'Connell reached the crossroad, the snowy countryside sparkled with sunlight. Only minutes before, the cloudless sky seemed like Kate's world—warm and wonderful. But now a cold wind crept into her heart. Worry darkened her deep blue eyes.

I'll find Anders, she decided, flipping her long braid over her shoulder. *He'll know what to do.*

Ahead of Kate, the road led past a brickyard, then up a steep hill. On that January day in 1907 her brother and Erik Lundgren were harvesting ice for the Trade Lake Creamery. If Kate found them, maybe she could talk to Anders.

Just then two draft horses appeared at the top of the hill. Their large bodies strained forward into the harness. Huge blocks of ice filled the sleigh behind them.

A tall boy walked alongside, holding the reins. A warm cap covered his brown hair, but Kate recognized him and his horses, Queen and Prince.

"Erik!" she called.

A grin broke across his face. "Hi, Kate!"

As Queen and Prince started down the hill, they picked up speed. The load shifted. Heavy blocks of ice crashed against the front of the sleigh. A brace snapped, and a plank flew off. Ice tumbled onto the heels of the horses.

Queen snorted in terror. Prince leaped ahead.

Erik tugged on the reins. Leaning back, he pulled with all his strength. But the horses yanked him along. Hitting a patch of ice, he slid beside the sleigh.

Kate gasped. If Erik fell, he'd be dragged. The sleigh might even run over him.

In the next instant a rein snapped. Sensing her freedom, Queen tossed her head. A moment later the second rein snapped. Queen and Prince bolted, out of control.

Erik ran after them. But the horses flattened their ears and picked up speed. Without swerving, they headed straight toward Kate.

Her heart pounding, she stared at the runaways. Her feet felt frozen to the ground.

Help! she wanted to cry. But no sound came. Unable to think, she knew only that she'd be trampled.

"Kate!" Erik shouted.

As though from far away, she heard his voice, but panic held her motionless. The horses loomed closer, driven by fear.

"Kate! Get out of the way!"

To her surprise, her legs worked. Leaping out of the road, she tumbled into a mound of snow.

Seconds later, the horses thundered past. With the sleigh swaying behind, they headed for the village of Trade Lake.

"Runaway!" Erik shouted the warning.

As Kate pulled herself from the snow, Erik tore past, calling again. "Runaway!"

But the horses raced down the main street. Near Trader Carlson's store, people fled inside. At the creamery the team rounded the corner, still going full speed. The sleigh swung wide, skidding out, but Queen and Prince kept on. Then the creamery blocked Kate's view.

Stopping at the corner, Erik gazed up the road toward Mission Church. For a long moment he stood there. When he shook his head, Kate knew the horses must be out of sight.

Pulling off a mitten, Kate wiped the snow from her face. Her hand trembled. *Will I ever get used to living here?* she wondered.

Ten months before, her widowed mother had married Anders's father. Kate and Mama had moved from Minneapolis to northwest Wisconsin. There they had become part of the Nordstrom family of Papa, Anders, nine-year-old Lars, and five-year-old Tina. In Kate's new life there always seemed to be something that frightened her.

I don't want to be afraid, she thought now. Ever since she'd been here, things had gone wrong around Windy Hill Farm. In that third week of January, Papa Nordstrom worked far away in a logging camp. In two or three months Mama's baby would be born. And Lars? Off and on for several weeks he'd been sick. And the worst part of winter could still be ahead.

Bending down, Kate brushed snow from her coat and long stockings. *No matter what happens, I want to be*—She thought a moment. Brave seemed a strange word. *Courageous?* That seemed to fit some great hero, not her, Kate O'Connell, newly turned thirteen.

By the time Erik walked back to her, Kate stood as tall as her short height allowed. But her knees felt weak.

"You all right?" he asked, looking scared.

Kate nodded, still too shaken to speak. When at last she found her voice, she asked, "Are *you* all right?" She'd never seen Erik's face so white.

"Yup," he said, flexing his shoulders. "I'll be sore, but I'm fine. It wasn't fun seeing Queen and Prince head your way."

Kate shivered. "I was so scared I couldn't move. Thanks for yelling." Even now her voice trembled.

Erik gazed back up the hill. Blocks of ice lay scattered along the road.

"C'mon," he said at last. "Let's get some hot cocoa. You'll feel better." But he looked as though he needed encouragement himself.

When Kate and Erik reached the Trade Lake Creamery, the buttermaker stood in the doorway. "Your horses, weren't they, Erik? Did you get hurt?"

Erik shook his head.

"That's good. Could have been a bad one." Mr. Bloomquist

was young and short and stocky. As he leaned against the frame building, a friendly smile lit his face. "Better come in and warm up."

"Kate needs to," said Erik. "I'll go after my horses."

"Won't do you a bit of good," said the buttermaker. "By now they're most of the way home."

Erik sighed. "I suppose you're right." He still seemed unable to believe what had happened. "I lost the whole load. It shifted on that hill."

"You shouldn't be using that hill," said the buttermaker. "Usually the men avoid it." Then he seemed to notice Kate's trembling. "Are you hurt?"

Kate shook her head, but her teeth chattered.

"My horses almost ran her down," Erik explained.

"Like I said, you shouldn't be using that hill. Maybe that's what comes from accepting Fenton's bid. The creamery doesn't usually give the job of harvesting ice to a newcomer."

Again Mr. Bloomquist turned toward Kate. "Come in and get warm."

Kate followed Erik and the buttermaker into a large open room. On one side, farmers brought in their milk cans. The buttermaker separated the whole milk and kept the cream. Then the farmers took the skim milk back home with them.

Nearby, in the center of the room, was something that looked like a big wooden barrel resting on its side. Kate knew it must be the butter churn.

Beyond that, a man came through a doorway. Before the door swung shut, Kate noticed a one-foot wall.

"That's the cold room," Erik said, as though he'd guessed Kate's question. "The creamery uses the ice we harvest to cool cream and store butter."

Mr. Bloomquist led them into a smaller room with a large round tank on top of a high brick wall. Opening a door in the wall, Mr. Bloomquist threw in three-foot logs.

Through small holes in another door, Kate saw flickering flames. Pulling off her mittens, she held out her hands to warm them. As she felt the welcome heat, her usual curiosity returned. "What is it?" she asked Erik.

"The tank? A steam boiler. It heats water for the steam engine." He tipped his head toward a shiny bronze cylinder nearby. "Creamery uses steam for all its cleaning and power."

A few minutes later the buttermaker returned to the larger room, closing the door behind him. Erik reached for a glass jar he had set near the boiler. Unscrewing the lid, he offered the contents to Kate. "You first."

Kate's fingers felt warmer, just holding the jar filled with hot liquid. But then she tasted the cocoa. "It's sour!" she exclaimed, making a face.

Erik laughed, as though relieved to find something funny. "Sorry! It's been warming up all day. Now if it was up to Anders, he'd drink it anyway."

For a moment Kate thought about her stepbrother. Before Christmas he'd sprained his ankle. By now he was using that foot again. Yet Kate felt glad he wasn't around when the horses ran away. He might not have been able to escape.

Sitting down on the floor, Kate leaned back against the warm bricks. As her trembling stopped, she noticed small bottles and what looked like test tubes on a nearby desk. "What are those?" she asked.

Erik grinned. "You're feeling better, I can tell. Anders would call you Curious Kate."

"But I really want to know."

"Maybe it's a mystery you'll have to solve."

"Oh, come on. *You* tell me."

Erik laughed, but explained anyway. "When farmers bring in their cans of milk, the buttermaker uses those tubes to take samples. The higher the butterfat, the more we get paid for our cream."

The mention of money triggered a thought and Kate asked, "Did you know the cream checks were stolen last night?"

Erik's eyes no longer teased. "Heard about it when I came to work this morning. First time we ever missed a check."

"We need that money," said Kate, her voice low.

"So do we," answered Erik. "Every farmer does. Mighty hard not to get money we count on."

Kate sighed. That morning she'd walked three miles to pick

up her family's check and buy cloth. The baby Mama expected was getting bigger every day. Even Mama's largest dress stretched tight across her stomach.

And that wasn't all. Soon they'd need flannel to sew little clothes for the baby.

"I went to Gustafson's store," Kate said. "Everyone was talking about the stolen checks. They all said, 'Never before! We've never had such a robbery in northwest Wisconsin!' But it happened."

"The creamery will stop payment on the checks," Erik told her.

"And then what?" Kate wanted to know.

"They'll reissue them."

"What do you mean, *reissue* a check?" asked Kate.

"Write it out again. Trouble is, we have to wait till that happens. And there's something I don't understand. Why would someone steal *checks*? They can't cash 'em around here. If the thief tried, everyone would know who he is."

Standing up, Erik shrugged into his coat. "I have to get back to the lake."

"Can I come with you?" Kate asked. "I want to watch, and maybe I can talk to Anders."

As she pulled on her coat, she heard voices through the door into the larger room.

"I took care of the checks," someone said.

Kate strained to hear, but couldn't catch the quiet answer.

"I could write out new checks tonight." That was the first man speaking again. Then Kate heard only the word *ledger*.

"What's a ledger?" she whispered.

"A record book." Erik was listening too. "For keeping track of the cream farmers bring in."

"I got hold of Sheriff Saunders," the first voice went on. "He'll do everything he can."

"That's Andrew Anderson number 3 talking," Erik whispered.

"Number 3?" asked Kate.

"Because of all the Andrew Andersons. Helps us know which one. Shhh!"

Mr. Anderson's voice sounded heavy with worry. "The thief knew my routine. He knew what night of the month I made out checks and where I put them."

A chair scraped across the floor. As footsteps approached the door between the two rooms, Erik moved quickly through another door leading outside.

Kate followed him. "Who's Andrew Anderson number 3?" she asked when they were safely away from the building.

"You know him. Goes to our church. High forehead, long flowing beard."

As they reached the hill where the ice broke loose, Erik looked around. "Mr. Anderson used to be postmaster. Now he's secretary-treasurer of the creamery." Finding the plank from the sleigh, Erik set it at the side of the road.

"And secretary of the Trade Lake Fire Insurance Company?" For Kate it was all falling into place.

"Yup," Erik said. "Papa says Mr. Anderson is a good man and a careful manager. The creamery and insurance company have done well, mostly because of him."

On the other side of the hill, Kate and Erik left the road.

"You know what's really strange?" Erik continued. "No one even knew that Mr. Anderson had a hiding place for the checks. But the thief found them the one night of the month they were there."

Inside her mittens Kate's fingers clenched, just thinking how Mr. Anderson must feel. With all her heart she wanted to solve the robbery. Yet she knew that someone willing to steal from a creamery might be dangerous.

"If no one knows who took the checks—" Kate stopped, afraid to say what she thought.

But Erik finished for her. "The thief can steal from the creamery again."

2

Trouble at Trade Lake

*K*ate's stomach knotted. "He can steal any time he wants."

"Any time at all," answered Erik.

Kate didn't like that idea. It was bad enough not getting a check today. When *would* they get paid? All the farmers in the area depended on the income from the creamery.

"But you and Anders will get money for harvesting ice," she said.

"Maybe." Erik looked gloomy. "If the creamery can't pay the farmers, how can they pay us?"

Kate and Erik headed across a field partly cleared of trees. Horses and sleighs had packed down a trail to Little Trade Lake.

Erik started walking faster. "I need to hurry. Mr. Fenton's not going to like it that I lost a load of ice."

Soon they passed through a stand of pine trees. Beyond that, deep snow made it difficult to tell where the shore ended and the lake began.

At the center of the bay a patch of cleared ice sparkled in the afternoon sunlight. A sleigh and team of horses waited near a hole of black water.

On the far side of the opening, someone had marked squares

in the ice. A man was using a long saw to cut the squares into blocks.

"It looks like a checkerboard," said Kate. "But it's also like a cake. How do they get out the first piece?"

Erik grinned. "Curious Kate again." Just the same, he told her. "They push the block down and shove it under the ice."

A moment later his grin disappeared. "Well, wish me luck with Mr. Fenton!"

As Kate waited well out of the way, Erik started toward a man holding a long pole. Using the point on the end, the man pushed blocks of ice through a channel of dark water.

LeRoy Fenton, thought Kate. The day before he'd hired Erik and Anders to fill in for men who were sick.

Kate spotted her brother nearby. A shock of blond hair stuck out from beneath a knitted cap. His broad shoulders stretched the seams of his jacket. With boots planted on the edge of the hole, he held out large tongs.

A man wearing a red and black plaid mackinaw stood next to him. "C'mon, c'mon," he said, his gravelly voice impatient.

As Anders reached out over the water, Kate caught her breath. The ice was wet and slippery.

Then she saw a wide band around the toes of her brother's boots. Short roofing nails, poked through the bottom side of the band, gave his feet a grip. Catching a large block of ice, Anders tightened his tongs around it.

The man next to him also held tongs and closed them around the opposite side of the block. Together they pushed the ice deeper into the water. As it bobbed to the surface, they swung it onto the ice, then onto the sleigh.

"That's it," said the man. "All it can hold." He hooked a chain across the back of the sleigh, then waved the driver on.

Anders glanced toward Kate. Flexing his muscles, he grinned.

Show-off! Kate thought. Still, she felt proud of her brother.

When Anders saw Erik, his lopsided grin disappeared. "What's wrong?" he asked.

From near the channel of open water, Mr. Fenton looked up.

Seeing the boys, he called out, "Let's cut the talking and get back to work!"

"Sorry, Mr. Fenton," Erik said, walking over. "But I can't."

Like the man with Anders, Mr. Fenton wore four-buckle boots and a red and black mackinaw. He was of medium height and had a heavyset frame. His arms looked thick and strong.

"Where's your sleigh?" he asked Erik, his long pole still in hand. "We're ready to load."

Erik faced him. "I had a runaway."

"What's the matter, lose control of your horses?"

Erik's chin shot up. "The ice shifted on that steep hill near the creamery."

"And how long have you handled horses?" Mr. Fenton's voice sounded smooth as cream.

Erik straightened, seeming to grow taller. "Since I was nine years old, sir."

"Taking your team too fast, were you?"

A flush of red crept across Erik's face. "No, Mr. Fenton."

Erik's voice still sounded polite, but Kate knew he was angry.

"Queen and Prince started down the hill the way horses always do," Erik said. "A front brace broke. When the plank fell off, blocks of ice hit the horses' heels. They spooked."

By now the man working with Anders had turned toward Erik to listen. The same height and build as Mr. Fenton, the second man had a black beard trimmed close to his face. Mr. Fenton's mustache and hair were the color of sand.

"Well, see what your poor handling has done for us," Mr. Fenton said, as though he hadn't heard Erik. "Without a sleigh to load, we can't take out more ice."

"I know, Mr. Fenton. I'm sorry."

"Sorry! Lot of good that does!"

Erik bit his lip as though trying hard to keep from snapping back. He glared toward Anders, and a look of understanding passed between them.

As Mr. Fenton talked on, Erik again looked him straight in the eye. Finally the man summed up his complaints. "That's what happens when we hire children to work for us."

Erik's flush deepened, yet he managed not to speak.

But Anders stepped forward, directly in front of Mr. Fenton. "You're not being fair!" he exclaimed. "It's your fault the accident happened."

"*My* fault?" Mr. Fenton's eyes looked dangerously cold.

Anders held his ground. "Your fault," he repeated. "For saying we have to use that hill."

"You remember, Anders, that I'm the boss around here." Once again Mr. Fenton's voice sounded smooth.

But the tall blond boy kept on. "Old-timers avoid a steep hill if they can. If we harvested ice on Hidden Lake we wouldn't have to go over that hill."

This time it was Mr. Fenton who flushed red. "Who do you think you are, telling me what to do? You're just a boy."

"A boy who gives you a full day's work," Anders said, and Kate knew he was beyond stopping. "A boy who works just as well as a man."

"A boy who gives me a lot of lip, you mean. I don't have to take that."

The cold January air felt heavy with anger. Anders opened his mouth and just as quickly closed it. An uneasy look flashed across his face.

Be quiet, Anders! Kate wanted to cry out. *What about the money we need?* Would her brother lose the only paying job available to him?

As Anders drew a deep breath, Kate wondered if he remembered. "I'm sorry," he said, the words coming from deep inside.

Mr. Fenton smiled. "I can forget your poor manners if you stop telling me what to do." He reached out to shake Anders's hand as though the matter were settled.

But Anders stood with arms at his side, hands balled in fists. His face looked stony with anger.

Slowly Mr. Fenton dropped his hand. When he spoke again, he sounded as if nothing had happened. "Well, by the time the other sleigh gets back, it'll be dark. We're going to have to call it a day." He looked around at the man sawing blocks of ice. "No work tomorrow," he called.

Kate saw panic on her brother's face. She guessed what he was thinking. No work? No money?

Mr. Fenton glanced toward the man who worked with Anders. "Both Gunnar and I have other work to do. But if the weather holds, be back the day after." His look included Anders and Erik.

Quickly Anders picked up his tongs, hiding whatever relief he felt. He and Erik set off on the trail leading to the road. When they reached Kate, she fell into step behind.

As soon as they entered the grove of trees, Anders spoke. "Of all the—"

"Shhh!" Erik warned in a low voice. "Sound carries. He might hear."

His face straight ahead, Anders stalked the rest of the way through the pines.

They were almost to the Trade Lake Creamery before Kate spoke of the robbery. "What should we do about Mama and the baby?" she asked. "How are we going to buy the things we need?"

Anders didn't seem too concerned. "The creamery will write out new checks. They'll have 'em tomorrow. Or the next day."

"Did they tell you that?" asked Kate.

"No, but they will."

"They didn't tell me either," Kate said. Once Papa had told her that the men who ran the creamery were really wise. Yet she felt uneasy.

Anders turned to Erik. "Fenton didn't even ask if you got hurt."

"I didn't." Erik grinned. "After all, I've been handling horses since I was nine years old." Then his voice softened. "But Kate got a good scare."

"Well, you know about Kate." Anders talked as if she weren't there. "She's a scaredy-cat anyway."

"No, I'm not!" Kate sputtered.

"Kate had good reason to be afraid," Erik said. As they started up the hill toward Mission Church, he told the story.

Anders grew even more angry. "Old-timers use Hidden Lake for harvesting ice," he said.

"Where's that?" asked Kate.

"Back in the woods." Erik pointed to a trail ahead. Leading

off the road to their left, the track wound between swampy land back of the creamery and a cemetery farther up the hill.

"Hidden Lake has a bay close to the creamery," Erik continued. "That's where the men usually harvest ice."

"Until this year," Anders said. "Until LeRoy Fenton came to town in October."

"Who *is* Mr. Fenton, anyway?" Kate asked.

Anders shrugged. "A man who always acts like Mr. Smart. Came from another creamery somewhere. Applied for the buttermaker's job, but Mr. Bloomquist got it."

"So Mr. Fenton works for the buttermaker?" Kate asked.

"Part time," said Anders. "And Fenton got the bid for harvesting ice. Old-timers grumbled, but the job usually goes to the lowest bidder."

Soon they came to Mission Church with its two front doors, one for women to enter, the other for men. Anders turned to Erik. "Doesn't it bother you? Though he's new around here, Fenton acts like he knows everything."

"But isn't he the boss?" asked Kate.

"Yup, and it's all right if he bosses *us* around." Her brother's voice sounded like a growl. "But if Papa was here, Fenton wouldn't get away with what he's doing."

After walking on the road for a time, they cut across a field, then passed into woods.

"Sure miss your horses, Erik," Anders said. Even with shortcuts, it was a long walk to Windy Hill Farm.

"Hope I find 'em when I get home," Erik replied. Like Papa Nordstrom, Erik's father worked in a logging camp, but he had left his team of horses behind.

"When Mr. Fenton makes you work on Little Trade Lake, why do you use that steep hill?" asked Kate. "There's another way where the land is flatter."

Anders snorted. "Yah, sure!"

But Erik explained. "It's flatter and easier. But it's swampy there."

"Like here?" asked Kate.

"No, this is worse," Erik told her. As he spoke, they crossed onto the southwest end of Rice Lake. "There are floating bogs here. The water is much deeper."

Kate still didn't understand. "But it's winter. Isn't Little Trade Lake frozen?"

"Not where it's swampy. Get an early snow, and it keeps the water from freezing. The way in could have been solid ice if we'd known we were going to harvest there."

"You betcha!" said Anders. "We could have stomped down the grass and snow early in winter. It would have frozen hard. Or we could have tramped it down on a cold day. A trail would solid up pretty fast, just like here."

"But LeRoy Fenton didn't do that," explained Erik. "The first horses that tried to go in broke through."

"Through the ice?" asked Kate.

Anders snickered. "Mr. Grouch was driving."

"Mr. *Grouch*?"

"Gunnar Grimm. The man I worked with. Grouch, grouch, grouch all day long. Never talks when I ask him questions."

Kate remembered the other man in a red and black mackinaw. Heavyset and about the same height as Mr. Fenton, Gunnar Grimm lifted the huge blocks of ice with little effort.

"Yup," said Anders. "Mr. Grouch got the team out, but he never should have gone there in the first place. An old-timer wouldn't have. All I know is, I'm going to keep on eye on Mr. LeRoy Fenton."

"And on Hidden Lake?" asked Kate, half teasing.

"And on Hidden Lake," Anders answered. He still sounded angry.

3

Going Fishing

$\mathcal{O}$n her way to the barn the next day, Kate stopped in the chicken coop. Eager for their meal of warm mush, the chickens clustered around.

One old rooster, Big Red, tipped his head and cast his beady eyes toward Kate. Watching him, she laughed. "So you think this is your territory!"

As Kate filled the water container, the rooster's long beak darted forward. Just in time Kate jumped aside, avoiding his peck.

"You're a mean one!" she exclaimed. Carefully she edged out the door, making sure she kept her distance.

Soon after lunch, Erik came to the Windy Hill farmhouse.

"What happened to Queen and Prince?" asked Kate when she saw him.

"I found them munching hay, as peaceful as you please. Mama was mighty glad to see me walk in."

Kate remembered her terror of the day before. Even now, thinking about the runaway horses seemed like a nightmare.

"You know what?" Erik sounded as innocent as his face looked. "Maybe we ought to go fishing."

Anders agreed so quickly that Kate guessed the boys were planning to look around.

"We could use some fish for supper," Mama said. Today her golden blond hair fell in ringlets around her face.

Erik winked at Kate. "Better come with. You can bait the hooks."

Kate wrinkled her nose at him. She knew what some of the bait looked like. Worms that Anders and Erik had picked from the rotted wood of a dead tree. She'd do her best to use another kind of bait—small bits of pork rind saved from the last butchering.

Just the same, Kate wanted to go along. So did her younger brother Lars. After watching him fight colds most of the winter, Kate felt relieved to see him well enough to go.

As they put on their skis, Mama poked her head out the door. "Sure your ankle can handle it, Anders?"

"I'll be careful," he told her. It was the first time Anders had tried skiing since spraining his ankle before Christmas. He grinned at Mama. "Kate can bring me back if I don't make it."

Each one carrying something, the four of them skied down the hill near the farmhouse. Anders used a pole when skiing. The rest went without.

"Going to show you my favorite fishing hole," Anders told Kate. He looked like a small boy about to reveal a secret.

But Kate guessed where they were headed. "Hidden Lake?"

At the bottom of the hill, they followed a well-packed trail. Straight ahead through the woods was the school they'd attend when spring term started. Some schools closed just during the worst part of winter. But Spirit Lake School wouldn't reopen until April 8.

As Anders led them onto the ice of Rice Lake, he held out his ski pole. Made of a thin sapling stripped of bark, the pole had a point at the bottom end. The top was broader and easy to hold.

"See that area, Kate?" Anders pointed toward the southeastern bay. "Don't ever ski there."

Kate grinned. "I suppose the bogeyman will get me."

"Worse than that," Anders growled.

"Worse? What could possibly be worse?"

"Kate, my little sister, when Papa left, he told me to take care of you."

Kate giggled at his serious tone. "Oh sure, big brother. Just because you're taller, you can't boss me around. We're the same age."

Anders scowled. "There's a crick coming in on that side. And spring holes."

"Spring holes?" Kate still didn't take him seriously. When it came to teasing, Anders had gotten the best of her more than once.

"Spring holes."

Kate glanced at Erik and Lars. Neither one of them grinned.

"Big round holes," said Anders. "Holes made by springs. The ice never freezes, no matter how cold it gets. There can be a foot or two of snow just resting on top of the water."

Kate squinted her eyes, trying to see. The southeastern bay stretched away, smooth and peaceful in the afternoon sunlight.

"Once when the snow was deep like this, I tried skiing across that part of the lake," Anders went on. "I was going along lickety-split and stretched out my pole." Swinging his pole ahead, he showed her. "The pole dropped down. There was nothing there."

Kate swallowed hard. It wasn't difficult to guess what might have happened.

Avoiding the creek that let out of the southwest end of the lake, they stayed on a packed-down trail through the boggy area.

"Just remember, Kate," said Anders. "If you come through alone, this is the only safe place to cross."

For a time they followed the road to Trade Lake. Then Erik took the lead, breaking trail through a woods. Their wide skis held them up, even in deep snow.

Soon they came to a large open space. Anders and Erik looked around, and so did Kate. On this side of the lake the land sloped gradually down to where water would lie in summer. Across the bay, however, the shore rose to a steep, forested hill and farm-land beyond.

Except for animal tracks, the snow was unbroken. With only trees and hills in sight, the place seemed harmless. Why didn't

LeRoy Fenton want men working on Hidden Lake?

Erik put Kate's disappointment into words. "Nothing here to see."

But Anders skied onto the lake. "Well, we told Mama we'd fish. We better get started."

Facing the south shore, he stepped to the left and right, lining himself up with a large tree.

"Looking for something?" Kate asked.

"Yup. My favorite fishing hole."

Taking the ice chisel he carried, Anders cleared off the snow. With a long handle, the chisel had a narrow blade about two inches wide. "I suppose I have to make a hole for you, Kate," he said, and started chopping.

The sound rang out, breaking the stillness. Before long, the chisel splashed down into cold, dark water.

Lars took his turn next, then Erik, all making their own hole. Anders busied himself with a fishing line, then chopped a fourth hole for himself.

"C'mon, Kate, I'll show you how." He handed her a small board with grocery string wrapped around it, then dug into a can. When he held up a soft white worm, Kate stepped back.

Anders laughed. "Won't hurt you a bit, scaredy-cat!"

Erik grinned. "Maybe she'd like some pork rind instead."

Lars had already dropped a line through his hole in the ice. Before long he cried, "I've got something!"

Kate watched his string dip into the water. For a moment Lars let the line go, then jerked it up, setting the hook. As he pulled in the line, he wound it around the small board.

Suddenly the head, then the body and tail of a northern pike appeared through the hole in the ice.

"It's a big one!" cried Kate.

Erik and Anders surrounded the hole, ready to grab if the fish slipped off the hook. But the line held, and Lars swung it to safety, out over the snow. Proudly he held it up.

"Oh, wow!" exclaimed Kate.

Anders clapped his brother on the back. "That's a six- or seven-pounder!"

"It's over two feet long!" exclaimed Erik.

Lars's eyes glowed with excitement. "It's sure the biggest fish I've ever pulled in!"

"Well, let's see if the rest of us can catch up to Lars," Anders said as he let down his line.

Kate reached for a bit of pork rind, then remembered she wasn't going to be a scaredy-cat. Gingerly she poked into the can for a soft white worm. She picked one up so carefully that she dropped it twice.

Looking around, she saw Anders watching her. This time she took better hold of the worm. As she pierced it with her hook, the worm squished.

Kate bit her lip. Quickly she dropped her line through the hole in the ice.

A moment later she felt a tug. "I've caught something!"

"Aw, Kate," drawled Anders. "You can't have something that fast. Ever been fishing before?"

Kate shook her head. Just the same she watched her line, sure that something clung to the other end.

Erik came over to stand beside her. "Let it play with the bait a bit."

Kate loosened her hold, but the line didn't pull down the way it did for Lars. Instead, the string held tight and steady. When she tried to wind it up, the line refused to come.

"Just a minute, Kate." Erik stared into the hole. "Something's wrong."

By now Anders was watching. "Got a really big one?" Handing his line to Lars, he came over.

Pulling off his mitten, Erik felt Kate's line. "She's caught on something."

"In the middle of the lake?" Kate asked.

"Aren't any weeds around here," Anders said. He, too, took hold of the line and pulled gently but firmly. "She's caught all right."

Erik knelt down. Slowly he tugged, being careful not to break the line. But the string held fast.

"Let me try," said Anders. When he pulled again, the string seemed to come free, but Anders could pull it only two or three feet.

From opposite sides of the hole, Anders and Erik tugged once more. Another foot of line came up, dragging something with it.

"A chain!" exclaimed Kate. "It's caught on the links!"

"Well, little sister," Anders said. "For once you're right!"

Reaching into the dark water, Erik grabbed hold of the chain. "Get the ice chisel," he said. "Hurry!"

Quickly Kate slid the long handle through the loop Erik held. Lying across the hole, the handle of the chisel kept the chain from dropping back into the water.

Pulling hand over hand, Anders brought up more of the chain.

"There's something hooked to it!" cried Lars, who had taken in the other fishing lines.

"Yah betcha, old buddy," Anders replied. "Something too big for this hole."

"What is it?" asked Kate.

Anders shrugged. "Whatever it is, we have to make a bigger hole. For that we need the ice chisel. Where's my ski pole?"

As Anders hung on to the chain, Erik slipped the pole through the loop and freed the ice chisel. Then the boys started widening the hole.

When Kate took her turn chopping, she saw something bobbing about two feet beneath the surface. "It's shiny metal," she said.

More than once Kate and the boys stopped to tug on the chain. Each time one of them went back to using the chisel.

At last Anders put it down. "Let's try again."

He and Erik knelt down on either side of what was now a good-sized hole. As Erik pulled the chain, Anders reached out. For a moment nothing happened. Then Erik gave another yank. This time a five-gallon milk can bobbed into view.

When Anders tried to grab it, the can slipped out of his hands. "It's too heavy for a can that size, even if it was full." He leaned back to think about it.

Again Erik yanked hard on the chain. This time a handle appeared above the water. Kate grabbed for it and lifted. But it took Anders's strong arms to swing the can onto the ice.

Chains attached to the handles on either side reached down to the chain on which Kate's line had caught. That chain led down into the dark water.

Once more Erik grabbed the ice-cold links. Hand over hand he pulled until something heavy rose to the surface. With a mighty tug he lifted out a snarl of wire wrapped around a good-sized rock.

"No wonder it's so heavy!" Erik exclaimed.

"Quite a catch!" said Kate.

"For a first-timer, you're not bad!" Anders told her. "But what's a milk can doing down in the lake?"

"Is it watertight?" she asked.

"If the lid's pressed down hard," Erik told her. "Whoever took care of this one made sure."

Two ropes, with ends tied to the handles on either side, crossed the top of the can in an X. The lid looked as secure as someone could make it.

Who would bury a milk can in the icy waters of a lake? What was inside?

4

Discovery!

*K*ate pulled off her mittens to untie the knots that held the cover of the milk can in place. Ice was forming on the rope. Soon it would freeze solid.

The cold bit into Kate's hands, numbing them. As her fingers stiffened, they grew clumsy. Already a skim of ice coated the top of the can.

"Where's your knife, Anders?" she asked.

Her brother patted his pockets and pulled it out. As Anders cut the rope, Erik yanked off the lid.

Lars reached into the can. "A gunnysack!" He held it up for them to see. A stout string held the sack shut.

Erik helped Lars untie the string. All of them peered inside the sack.

Lars's blue eyes danced. Erik let out a long whistle. Kate felt her heart leap into her throat.

"I thought so!" Anders exclaimed.

It was Kate who took out slips of paper. "Checks from the Trade Lake Cooperative Creamery!"

Anders reached for another handful and read the names aloud. "This one's for Josie's father, Henry Swenson. And here's your father, Erik."

"And Papa?" asked Kate, looking through the checks she held. "Elroy Johnson. Stanley Sundquist. Here it is! Carl Nord-strom."

Lars's grin spread from ear to ear. "It's the loot from the rob-bery, all right!"

In that moment Kate felt uneasy. Lars's words made their discovery real. With that reality came her awareness of danger. Looking over her shoulder, she asked, "So what do we do?"

Anders returned the money to the gunnysack. Erik retied it, slipped the sack into the can, and replaced the lid. Like Kate, he, too, glanced around.

The hidden lake seemed still and serene, but Anders put their feeling into words. "We're sitting ducks out here. If anyone comes this way, he'll spot us in a second."

"Let's get off the ice," Kate said.

Again they looked around, but this time for a hiding place. On the north end of the bay, tall bent-over grass marked a swampy area. On a second side, the shore rose steeply. Climbing with the milk can and heavy rock would be difficult. But on the south side of the bay, near the place where they skied in, the ground sloped gently upward.

"What about over there?" asked Kate.

"If we could just get rid of this big rock," said Anders. Yet the chain and the wire around the rock were frozen together.

"Can't destroy evidence, anyway," Erik replied.

With Anders carrying the milk can and Erik the rock, they left the ice for the cover of trees.

"Got any ideas?" Anders asked as he set the can down.

"We have to get help," said Kate.

"I know, I know." Anders sounded impatient. "But what do we do with the milk can? If we take it to the creamery, the whole town will see us walking through Trade Lake."

"The whole town—and maybe the thief," said Kate. With each minute she felt more aware of what a dangerous thing they had found.

"So we can't go to the creamery," Lars decided. Surrounded by freckles, his blue eyes looked serious.

"You got it, brother!" Anders replied. "Maybe we should split up—two of us go, two of us stay here."

But Erik glanced at Kate and Lars. "We're sticking together," he said. He sounded as if he wouldn't even consider another idea.

"Where can we hide the can while we go for help?" Kate asked.

Backing off from where they stood, Erik looked along that side of the shore. "There's a brush pile." He pointed. "But we've got a bigger problem."

Kate knew what he meant. "Our tracks in the snow. They'll lead someone right to the milk can."

Then she noticed the light slanting across the slope. Soon the hill would be cold and dark. "We have to decide," she said.

Glancing toward the sun, Anders looked worried. "That brush would do it, so let's cover our tracks."

Leaving the can on the shore, they returned to the fishing holes. Anders and Erik put on their skis and started back to the slope. Lars collected his fish, the lines, and bait, and skied to the place where they'd come in to the lake.

Kate tromped down the snow, hiding the deep round circle left by the bottom of the milk can. There was nothing to do with the large hole in the ice but hope that it would freeze over soon.

Stepping into her skis, Kate picked up the ice chisel and followed Anders and Erik to the shore. Using the two-inch blade, she smoothed out the round mark left by the can.

With Anders carrying the milk can and Erik the rock, they skied close to the pile of brush. Slipping one foot from his ski, Erik stretched out and set down the milk can. Anders handed him the rock, and Erik hid that also. Reaching still farther, Erik pulled branches over the can, the rock, and his boot print.

When all of them joined Lars, dusk was upon them. As Kate looked around, she saw no one. Perhaps the lake was well named, and they were safely hidden.

"We have to decide who to tell," Anders said. "The thief could be most anyone."

Kate felt scared. "Are you saying we could look right at him and not know it?"

"Yup!" Anders offered his lopsided grin. "Now think about

that for a minute! Just think how exciting your life can become."

But Kate didn't like that idea at all. Then she caught the look in Lars's eyes. Always he'd been more tender than Anders. Talking to a thief didn't seem a joke for him either.

"It's not funny, Anders," said Kate, tipping her head toward her younger brother.

"Just letting you know the risks," Anders replied. But he caught Kate's signal. His grin disappeared.

"So what can we do?" asked Erik. "Who do we trust?"

Kate felt at a loss. She trusted Mr. Swenson, Josie's father. But would he be the right person to tell?

"What about Mr. Bloomquist?" asked Lars. In the dusk his freckles stood out on his pale face.

"The buttermaker?" Anders thought about it. "He's new here. I don't know him very well." He looked at Erik. "Do you?"

Erik shook his head. "But we need someone connected with the creamery."

"Let's go to Andrew Anderson number 3," said Anders. "He's secretary-treasurer."

"You trust him?" Kate asked.

"Yah, sure," Anders told her. "With our lives!"

"Anders!" Kate exclaimed. "Stop teasing. It isn't funny!"

For once Anders looked dead serious. "I'm not teasing, Kate. Before Papa left, he told me to take care of you and Mama and Tina.

"And me too?" asked Lars.

"You, too, little brother." Anders winked. "But Kate's the biggest problem. The rest of you I can handle."

Kate sputtered, but Erik laughed. "Don't you worry about it, Anders. I'll help with Kate."

Anders grinned. "Like I said, mighty big problem that it takes two of us."

Before Kate could answer, Anders started back over the ice of Hidden Lake. "Just follow me. I'm your trusty guide through thick and thin. Through the cold of day and peril of night."

In spite of herself, Kate giggled. As she fell into line, she called ahead. "But, Anders, how do you know we can trust Mr. Anderson?"

Anders swung around. "Because Papa trusts him. Papa likes what he stands for. That's why he and Mama named me Anders."

Kate was surprised. She knew only that Anders's mother had died from illness, for Anders seldom spoke about her. Months later Anders's father had married her mother. During the time without one parent, Anders had taken on the responsibilities of an adult.

"Anders? After Andrew?" Kate asked.

"Yup, Anders is Swedish for Andrew. I'm named after the Andrew in the Bible, but also Andrew Anderson number 3. That's why I'm so great!"

In the twilight Kate caught his grin. Knowing they'd soon be surrounded by total darkness, she skied quickly. Lars followed her, and Erik brought up the rear.

After a time Kate called out. "How far, Anders?"

"His farm is north of Hidden Lake."

When they reached Mr. Anderson's house, Anders took off his skis and bounded up the steps. A tall thin man with a long flowing beard opened the door.

"I *do* know him!" Kate murmured under her breath. She remembered times when Mr. Anderson spoke up at church. More than once, he'd helped the congregation make wise decisions.

"Come in, come in," he said now. In the glow of a kerosene lamp, his hair and beard were a salt-and-pepper mixture of gray and white. His lined face looked kind.

As Kate felt the warmth of the wood stove, she realized how cold she had become. In spite of her wool stockings and mittens, her toes and fingers felt numb.

The Andersons were sitting down to supper, and Mrs. Anderson set on more plates. As soon as he said the blessing, Mr. Anderson turned to Anders. "Well, what can I do for you?"

As her brother told the story, Kate watched the older man. The expression in his quiet eyes changed from amazement to relief to joy. Standing up, he clapped Anders on the back. "Well, let's go after it. Let's rescue this milk can from beneath the brush."

In a minute he returned dressed in warm clothing. After lighting a farm lantern, he led them to the barn. Working together, they harnessed the horses.

"We'll get Harry Bloomquist," Mr. Anderson said as they climbed into the sleigh. "He's been working late at the creamery. He'll give an extra hand if we have any trouble."

As they drew up at the Trade Lake Creamery, Kate saw a kerosene lamp glowing through a window. Sitting at his desk, the buttermaker was working on some papers.

"Welcome," he said as they entered the small room with the steam boiler. "To what do I owe this great honor?"

"We've got good news for you, Harry." Mr. Anderson's eyes shone in the lamplight. "These young people found the checks!"

Enjoying every moment, Anders told what had happened. The story sounded even better on the second telling.

We can buy dress material for Mama, Kate thought as she listened to her brother. Maybe they'd even get cloth for baby clothes.

"We chopped a bigger hole and pulled out the can," Anders was saying when Kate heard a noise in the next room—a furtive noise, as if someone moved quietly. Tuning out her brother's voice, she listened.

"Where's the milk can now?" asked the buttermaker.

"Under a pile of brush on the south shore of Hidden Lake," Anders told him.

As Kate heard another sound, she remembered how easily voices carried between the two rooms. Erik, too, seemed to listen. As their gaze met, Kate tipped her head. Erik nodded. Quietly he edged toward the door into the large room.

Kate reached out for Mr. Anderson's farm lantern, picked it up, and followed. Just as Erik turned the doorknob, something crashed in the other room.

No longer cautious, Erik threw open the door. Kate followed with the lantern.

In the middle of the floor a milk can lay on its side. Erik grabbed the lantern from Kate. Its dim glow barely reached into the shadows, yet Erik held it out. Starting around one side of the room, he searched.

From somewhere beyond the large churn, Kate sensed a movement. "Over there!" she cried, pointing into the shadows.

In the light from the lantern two bright eyes shone from the dark.

5

Nighttime Search

*K*ate stepped back. What animal lurked in the shadows?

But Erik stalked ahead. A large orange cat bounded out. Kate jumped, then felt silly.

The cat streaked past her toward the buttermaker.

"False alarm!" Mr. Bloomquist exclaimed as he came into the room. "Tabby's our best mouser."

"False alarm?" Kate whispered to Erik. "I don't think so. I heard a door close."

"I don't think so either." Erik spoke softly.

The door to the cold room was a few steps beyond where the cat hid. Nearby was another door. Erik flung it open and hurried outside. As Kate followed, Anders and the men caught up.

Erik and Mr. Anderson started around the creamery in one direction. Kate and Anders took another. Mr. Bloomquist checked out the trees behind the building. But no one was found hiding in the dark.

"Whatever it was is gone," said Erik when they came back together.

"*Whoever* it was, you mean," answered Kate. "The noises I heard weren't made by a cat."

"We're all getting a bit jumpy," Mr. Bloomquist said as they returned inside. "Better tell me the rest of the story, Anders."

Anders pushed back his shock of blond hair and spoke quickly. "Then we went for Andrew Anderson," he said.

As Mr. Bloomquist asked one question after another, Kate grew more and more uneasy. "Can't we go to the lake?" she finally asked.

The buttermaker reached for his coat. It took another few minutes to find a farm lantern and light it.

Outside, they climbed into the sleigh. Mr. Anderson took the trail back of the creamery. At Hidden Lake Kate and the boys put on their skis. In the deep snow they could make better time.

Carrying a lantern, Erik led them up the slope. The men trudged behind with the second lantern. More than once, Kate looked over her shoulder, glad that Mr. Anderson was along. What if the person who stole the checks watched from the darkness?

Skiing ahead of Kate, Lars looked tired. Instead of his usual quickness, he had trouble keeping up with the older boys.

As everyone reached the pile of brush, the half moon came out from under the clouds. Kate held the lantern, and Erik and Anders pulled away the branches.

Before long Kate knew something was wrong. "Where's the milk can?" she asked.

Without answering, the boys worked even more quickly. When they had moved every branch without finding anything, they had to give up.

"Are you sure you have the right place?" asked Mr. Bloomquist.

"I'm sure," Anders growled.

Erik looked even more upset. "I *know* this is where I put it!"

"Maybe there's another pile of brush," suggested Mr. Anderson. Leaving them, he walked down to the lake. Kate followed on skis.

Standing on the snow-covered ice, Kate and Mr. Anderson looked back up the slope, searching. The dim light made it difficult to see. Finding nothing else, they returned to the others.

"Are you *sure* this is where you hid the can?" the buttermaker asked again.

Anders's laugh sounded harsh in the cold night air. "This is the place. Are you wondering if we're playing a prank?"

"No, no," Mr. Bloomquist said quickly.

"We didn't plan a wild-goose chase." Erik sounded apologetic, but Kate knew he was angry. "We've been honest with you."

"I believe you," said Andrew Anderson simply. "I know you best, Anders, and I trust you. Someone didn't want us to find that milk can."

"That noise in the creamery," said Kate. "Even a big cat wouldn't tip over a milk can. They're too heavy."

Mr. Anderson nodded. "Good thinking, Kate."

"If that person heard us talking, he got here first," said Erik.

Again Mr. Anderson agreed. "We have to find out who's been here. Let's look around for tracks. And let's work quietly in case the thief is still nearby, listening."

Close to the pile of brush, the snow was too trampled to pick out boot prints. Anders, Mr. Anderson, and Lars used one lantern, while Kate, Erik, and the buttermaker searched with the other.

It was easy to find their ski tracks from the afternoon and also the tracks they'd made coming back. When they spread out in a circle around the pile of brush, Kate discovered boot prints.

Just then Anders called out from the opposite side. "Here's something!" Again boot prints led away into the woods.

"There's two people?" asked Erik. "That's strange."

Lars and Mr. Anderson followed Anders in one direction, while Kate, Erik, and the buttermaker took the other. Kate spotted one boot print, then the next. Of medium size, they were far apart, as though the person either ran or walked fast.

The three had gone for some distance when the lantern sputtered and died. Erik groaned. "It's out of kerosene!"

Mr. Bloomquist sounded just as upset. "I forgot to fill it! I'll go back for the other lantern."

As the buttermaker disappeared into the darkness, Kate spoke softly. "Erik, do you trust him?"

"I don't know," he whispered back. "Maybe it's because he's new at his job. But it's one delay after another. If we'd gone straight to the milk can, we'd have it now!"

Kate sighed. "Every minute we lose—"

"I know. The thief gets farther away."

Kate stared at the ground. "Maybe we can see without the lantern."

They stood in an opening between trees where the light was better. Erik pointed. "There's the next footstep. Let's give it a try."

Watching closely, they started around the west side of the lake. Soon a lacework of branches dimmed what light there was, and they had to stop.

Kate looked up to where the moon hid under the clouds. "I wish it were full."

When the buttermaker returned, he brought the others. The trail Mr. Anderson, Anders, and Lars had followed led off a short distance, then circled back to the hole in the ice. In the lantern light Mr. Anderson looked grim about the time they'd lost.

"If only we had Lutfisk with us," said Anders. "He'd find the thief in a minute." Named after the dried cod that Swedes eat at Christmas, the dog was a good tracker.

By now Lars trembled with cold. "Why don't you go back to the sleigh?" Kate told him. "You could warm up under that heavy horse blanket."

But Lars shook his head. As they set out again, he kept up with the others.

They continued around the side of the lake until the boot prints led up a steep hill. There they left their skis standing in a snowbank and trudged on.

Soon Kate's legs ached from walking through deep snow. When she thought she couldn't take another step, they came to a large clearing. As they started across, the moon broke free of the clouds.

On the other side of the clearing, a large pine looked dark against the night sky. The lower boughs stirred. Was someone behind that tree? Kate couldn't be sure.

Then, next to the pine, bushes moved. Fear leaped into Kate's throat.

Reaching out, she touched Erik's arm. "Shhh!" she whispered when he would have spoken. She pointed toward the large pine. "Is someone there?"

"Stay here!" he said in a low voice. Leaping forward, he broke into a run. Anders and the men followed.

After a moment so did Kate, still holding the lantern. Erik wanted her out of harm's way. She wanted to see what happened.

The deep snow slowed them down. Partway across the clearing, Erik stumbled and fell. For a moment he lay there, out of breath. By the time Kate reached him, he was up again, running toward the tree.

He and Kate and Anders reached it together. No one stood on the far side, trying to hide. But there were boot prints in the snow.

As Kate held out the lantern, all of them looked around. Near the bushes, they saw prints that faced the clearing.

"He was watching," said Kate with a shiver. "Watching for us. How long ago?"

Just then the wind stirred the bushes. There was no way to know.

Scouting around, Anders found tracks leading off, away from the pine. Erik took the lantern, and they followed the boot prints to an ice-covered road. There the tracks disappeared.

Again they split into two groups, and each took a direction. With only one lantern it was hard to find a place where someone stepped off the road.

Finally they had to stop searching. No track remained. The footprints had vanished into the night.

Anders groaned. "He got away! We found the money, then lost it!"

To Kate this seemed the biggest blow of all—to be so close and then fail. But Andrew Anderson number 3 encouraged them. "You did your best."

Anders wasn't satisfied with that. "We should have brought the milk can to you. We were afraid the thief would see us carrying it."

"You were right," said the older man. "You could have tipped off the thief. At least we know the checks are still in the area. I'll notify Sheriff Saunders. We'll start our search again."

Walking back through the woods, they picked up their skies, then returned to Mr. Anderson's sleigh. "Climb in," he told them. "I'll give you a ride home."

Lars's face looked pinched and white with cold. As he crawled under a heavy horse blanket, his entire body trembled.

Watching him shiver, Kate felt concerned. Already Lars had been sick too often this winter.

Near the creamery, Mr. Anderson slowed the horses. "With all that's happened, it'd be easy to forget the contest," he told the buttermaker. "We still want you to enter."

What contest? Kate wondered, as Mr. Bloomquist dropped off the sleigh.

Soon they left the road to cross Rice Lake. Kate moved forward to talk to Mr. Anderson. "When will the creamery give out new checks?"

His hands on the reins, Mr. Anderson turned partway. "I don't know," he said.

"You don't *know*?" Anders blurted out.

Mr. Anderson didn't seem offended. "I can't reissue checks until I know what amount they should be."

"The buttermaker keeps a record of that." Erik sounded puzzled. "He writes down how much cream each farmer brings in."

"That's right," said Mr. Anderson. "He puts the information on a daily work sheet, then in a ledger."

"Are you saying—" Erik stopped, as though the idea were too awful to go on.

But Anders jumped in. "Are you saying the thief stole the ledger?"

Mr. Anderson's flowing beard trembled in the wind. "We don't know where it is."

Even in the dim light Kate saw his face. The good man grieved for the farmers.

"What does the ledger look like?" she asked after a moment.

"It's a gray book with green corners. About nine by thirteen inches and two inches thick."

When the horses started up the hill to the Nordstrom farm,

Mr. Anderson spoke again. "There's something I need to tell you young people. From what I've learned about you tonight, you'll keep looking for the stolen checks."

"And the ledger," said Anders.

"But you have to promise me something." In the crisp night air Mr. Anderson's voice sounded deep and strong. "Don't try to catch the thief yourself. Come to me if you see something out of the ordinary."

He looked directly at Anders. "Do you promise?"

"I promise," said Anders solemnly, his voice low.

Mr. Anderson turned toward Erik, then Kate.

"I promise," each of them said.

Mr. Anderson sighed. "I wish you weren't involved in this. But whatever you do, take care of each other. The thief knows who you are. He'll be watching you."

6

Letter From Sweden

As Mr. Anderson drove into the farm-yard, Kate saw Mama looking out the window. Kate and Anders climbed down and unloaded the fishing lines and skis, as well as the big northern. Lars stumbled toward the house.

"See you tomorrow," Erik called, as Mr. Anderson continued on to the Lundgren farm. "Let's plan what to do."

When Kate and her brothers entered the kitchen, she saw the worry in Mama's face.

"Where have you been?" Mama asked. A golden curl tumbled onto her forehead. Then Mama saw Lars and forgot everything else. "Come here," she told him gently. "Come next to the stove."

By now the nine-year-old shook so hard he could not unbutton his coat. When Lars let Mama help, Kate guessed how terrible he felt.

"Show her my fish, Kate!" Lars spoke through chattering teeth.

As she held up the northern, Kate felt excited for her brother.

"That's the catch of the season!" said Mama, admiring the big fish. But Lars's lips were blue.

Mama shook her head, as though holding back the words she wanted to say. Was one fish worth having Lars sick?

Anders took out the scale. "Exactly seven pounds!" he told his brother, then measured the fish. "Twenty-nine inches long!"

In the cold night air the northern had frozen. Anders spread newspapers on the table and let the fish thaw enough to clean.

Under the thick dusting of freckles, Lars's skin looked paper white. Though Mama pulled off his boots and wrapped him in warm blankets, he continued to tremble.

Is it my fault? Kate felt uneasy. They'd been gone much longer than expected. *We should have made Lars stay at the creamery.*

"Have you eaten?" Mama wanted to know.

"At Andrew Anderson's," Kate said, and saw Mama's surprise. But instead of asking questions, her mother heated milk.

Even after drinking the warm liquid, Lars continued to shiver.

"I want you sleeping downstairs tonight," Mama told him. "We'll put the cot next to the wood stove in the dining room. You'll be warmer there."

Only after getting Lars settled did Mama sit down. Tall for a woman, she was usually slender. But now, beneath her apron, her rounded stomach looked large. "Tell me everything that happened."

As Anders cleaned the fish, Kate told the story.

"This Mr. Grimm?" asked Mama. "Who is he?"

"You mean Mr. Grouch," said Anders.

But Mama corrected him. "Don't call him by that name. Someday you'll slip and say it to his face."

Mama's blue eyes looked dark with worry. "I don't like this whole thing. Whoever the thief is, he's a dangerous man. You mustn't get mixed up with him."

Kate looked across the table at Anders. How were they going to find the checks if Mama didn't want them searching? And how could they look if Mama said no?

Anders seemed to read Kate's mind. "We don't want to get mixed up with him, Mama. Tomorrow Mr. Anderson will go to Grantsburg and talk to the sheriff. They're in charge. We just want to search for the milk can."

"I don't want either of you looking around." Mama sounded as if her mind was made up. "Anders, you take care of Kate."

Anders kept his face straight. "Sure, Mama. I'll watch out for my little sister. She always does what I say."

Kate choked, but managed to keep her mouth shut.

Mama pushed back her chair. "Papa would know what to do. I wish he were here."

"I do too, Mama," Anders said, his voice quiet.

Kate felt surprised. Since Papa returned to the logging camp, Mama had often had a lonesome look. Even so, she seldom admitted how much she missed Papa.

Pulling herself up, Mama took off her apron. The dress she planned to wear until the baby came already strained at the seams. How could she possibly use that dress another two or three months?

Yet without the creamery check, how could they buy cloth? If Anders got paid, it wouldn't be for a while. And they had no idea when Papa would come home, bringing his earnings with him.

Taking out the large copper wash kettle, Kate set it on the cookstove. Filling a pail at the outside pump, she went back and forth, dumping water into the kettle.

Anders set the washstand near the stove, then put wooden tubs on either side of the wringer. Placing two chairs close together, he set a third wash tub on them. Then he, too, carried in bucket after bucket.

Finally all three tubs were full. Overnight the water would warm up to room temperature.

Taking a bar of soap, Kate rubbed the clothes where they were dirty. By the time she finished, her shoulder muscles ached. But when she tumbled into bed, she lay awake, thinking about the day.

When at last she slept, Kate dreamed about a milk can. In dark waters, it bobbed up and down. She reached out. The can bobbed away. Again Kate reached out. Again the can slipped out of her grasp. Kneeling down, she strained forward. As she grabbed for a handle, she lost her balance and slipped into the icy lake. Still thrashing her arms, Kate woke up.

Tina had pulled all the quilts to her side of the bed. Shivering, Kate yanked them into place, then over her head. It was a long time before she felt warm.

When Kate went down for breakfast, darkness still surrounded the house. Mama had built a good fire in the cookstove. In the large copper kettle sheets and white clothes were boiling. Using a wooden stick, Kate lifted them into the first rinse water.

Working swiftly, Mama shaped bread dough into loaves, then started breakfast. Soon the kitchen filled with the aroma of bacon and eggs and Mama's brown bread.

As Tina slipped into her chair, Anders came in from milking the cows. "No oatmeal this morning," he teased Kate. With the cookstove going all day, they'd have Mama's good soup at noon.

When Lars joined them, he sneezed, and Kate felt scared.

Mama looked up. "Lars, are you coming down with another cold?"

Lars nodded and sneezed at the same time. Quickly he blew his nose. As he turned away from the table, his eyes watered.

"You stay inside today," said Mama. "You've been sick so much we're not going to take any chances."

Kate finished breakfast, then pushed sheets and white clothes through the wringer and into the bluing. As she separated the shirts and tablecloths for starching, Kate watched her mother.

Though the sun had not yet risen, Mama looked as though she'd been up all day. Her pretty face seemed lined with weariness. Before long she disappeared into her bedroom.

"Did she say what's wrong?" Kate asked Anders as he put on layer after layer of work clothes.

"She's probably tired," he answered, as though trying to shrug it off.

But Kate felt uneasy. "Mama never lies down during the morning. What'll we do if *she* gets sick?"

A few minutes later sleigh bells jingled outside the kitchen door. Pulling on her coat, Kate followed Anders into the farmyard. As Queen and Prince came to a stop, Erik jumped down. The morning air felt crisp and cold, but his smile warmed Kate's heart.

"I drew a map of all the lakes in the area," he said.

"So did I!" exclaimed Anders. "I thought, 'Whoever the thief is, he probably can't hide the milk can where he lives. So where would he go? To another lake!' "

"But there're an awful lot of lakes around here," Kate said. Though she'd lived in Burnett County for ten months, she still felt confused at times, trying to sort out the ponds, lakes, and rivers.

Pulling up the collar of his jacket, Erik turned away from the wind. "Lot of people harvesting ice for their farms right now. It'd be easy for someone to drop a milk can in."

"Just one problem," Kate said, wishing she didn't have to tell Erik. "Mama's upset. She doesn't want us looking around."

"Really?" Erik groaned. "But how can we find the thief if we don't look?"

Kate shrugged her shoulders. During the night she had thought it through. More than once she told herself, *But let's search anyway*. Yet she didn't want to disobey Mama.

"Aw, it won't hurt just to take a look," Anders said, as though he'd heard Kate's thoughts.

But Erik shook his head. "We better not." He spoke slowly, and Kate knew he didn't like the idea either.

Climbing onto the sleigh, Erik took up the reins. "Maybe your mother will change her mind." Yet he didn't seem to believe his own words.

Returning to the kitchen, Kate put the first load of clothes into a basket. *Lars*, she thought, as she took the basket outside. She wished she could wash away her scared feelings. Already this winter, a cold had settled in her brother's chest.

And Mama. Often she looked exhausted. Yet Kate suspected Mama's weariness came from more than the baby. Papa was far away, and Mama wanted him safely home.

Snapping the wrinkles from the clothes, Kate moved quickly. But the sheets froze before she could hang them on the line.

As her hands turned red and stiff, her thoughts went on. *The milk can. Where is it now? And where would a thief hide the ledger?*

At lunch time Kate set up a drying rack and hung wool stockings near the cookstove. After freezing in the cold wind, she now felt hot and tired. Yet she needed to use the warm soapy water to wash the kitchen floor and outhouse.

By the time Kate finished scrubbing, the sun slanted westward, and she remembered the mail. Anders and Erik would cut across Rice Lake instead of going past the box.

Kate pulled on her warm clothes and set out on the long walk to the main road and the mail box. To her delight she found two letters—one from Papa, the other from Sweden. *Mama will feel better now,* Kate thought, and walked fast all the way home.

Mama's eyes sparkled as she poured a cup of coffee. Pulling her favorite chair close to a kitchen window, she sat down to enjoy the news.

Usually Mama read Papa's letters to them, but this one was for her eyes alone. "He's well," she said, her soft lips curving in a smile. Folding the letter, she tucked it inside her apron pocket. She'd take it out often to read Papa's words again.

With a warm glow still in her eyes, Mama opened the letter from Sweden. As she read, the color drained from her face. When she reached the end, she dropped the letter to her lap as though wishing she didn't have to touch it.

"Get the picture," Mama said.

Kate felt afraid. She didn't have to ask what picture Mama meant. Hurrying into the dining room, Kate went to the trunk Mama brought from Sweden. On its flat top stood the picture Kate knew well.

Mama's parents sat in the center, surrounded by her five sisters and two brothers. The youngest sister held a framed photograph of Mama.

"So I could still be part of the family," Mama often explained. Soon after coming to America, she'd had the photo taken and sent to her.

Now, as always, Mama pointed to each person in the picture. When she came to the smallest boy, she paused. "My little brother, Ben. Only two years of age when I left the old country. A chubby little boy with fat cheeks and happy eyes."

Drawing a long breath, Mama turned the picture over, as though she couldn't bear to see it. Without another word, Mama covered her face with her hands. Her shoulders shook with sobbing, but no sound came.

"Mama, what's wrong?" asked Kate.

Not since Daddy O'Connell died had Kate seen Mama so upset. Her grief seemed even worse because Mama seldom cried in front of anyone.

Kneeling down by the rocking chair, Kate put her arm around her mother's shoulders. "Mama?"

When her mother did not speak, Kate tried again. "Mama?"

Still no answer came, and Kate swallowed around the lump in her throat. "Did someone die?"

Mama shook her head. "Oh, no!" she said at last. "But something terrible has happened."

7

Accident!

Once more Mama broke into sobs.

"Mama, what's so terrible?" Kate felt desperate. Then she heard a sound near the doorway.

Tina stood there, her eyes wide and scared. Behind Tina stood Lars. Mama didn't notice either of them.

"Papa?" asked Lars, his voice a hoarse croak. "Did something happen to Papa?"

His question seemed to reach Mama. "No, Lars. Papa is fine." Mama's voice sounded unsteady. "But my little brother isn't."

Reaching for a handkerchief, Mama wiped her eyes. "My little brother, Ben," she moaned. "He stole money from a shop-keeper and ran away."

With a long shudder she blew her nose. "Six months ago Ben ran away. All that time since, and I did not know."

"How old is he now?" asked Kate.

Mama had to think. "A boy of two when I left the old coun-try." She counted the years. "He's eighteen now. Nineteen this spring."

For a long time Mama sat in her rocking chair, looking out the window. Far across the horizon, the western sky turned gold and red, then gray and black. A log fell in the cookstove, and cold reached into the room.

Kate built up the fire, but Mama still sat in her chair. As though seeing some distant place, she stared into the dark.

When Anders came home from harvesting ice, he looked at Mama, then at Kate. "What's wrong?" he asked.

Kate answered for Mama. "Her little brother stole from a shopkeeper and ran away. No one knows where he is."

Mama drew a deep breath. Her eyes and nose were red with crying.

Aching for Mama's hurt, Kate looked at Anders. *And don't you dare act smart*, she wanted to say. She knew how her brother could tease.

But Anders surprised her. Going over to Mama, he put his big hand on her shoulder. "I'm sorry," he said, his voice gentle.

Mama tried to smile, and Kate knew that the simple words had helped her.

After supper and chores, Anders took out some pieces of old harness. Sitting down at the kitchen table, he riveted the pieces of leather together.

"What're you doing?" asked Kate.

"Making a harness for Lutfisk. If I hitch him to the sled, Tina can ride behind."

Tina looked up from her cornhusk doll. As she crawled onto her brother's lap, her white-blond hair wisped around her face. She started talking in Swedish.

Though Kate couldn't understand the words, she guessed what the little girl said. Tina could hardly wait for a ride behind her brother's dog.

I'll write a letter to Papa, thought Kate. In the dining room, she picked up a wooden pen with a metal point and dipped it into the inkwell.

  Dear Papa,

she wrote.

Kate stared at the paper. What could she tell him? How frightened she felt about all that had happened? *I'm thirteen now and shouldn't be afraid anymore.*

For a long time Kate sat there, wondering what to do. *I shouldn't be scared, but I am.* Then she decided what to write:

> *Yesterday we went fishing and Lars caught a 7-pound northern. Anders measured it, and it was 29 inches long! We ate most of it for supper tonight, and it tasted good. Mama said it was almost as tasty as lutfisk.*
>
> *I know you have to be gone, but I miss you. This morning Tina got up while it was still dark and crept down to the kitchen. She thought that if she made cookies for you, you'd come home sooner. When Mama found her, Tina had flour all across the floor. She ate at least half a cup of sugar.*
>
> *We are doing fine. We hope you are well.*

We hope you are well? The words sounded stiff, even to Kate. Too often she thought about Daddy O'Connell, and how he died in a construction accident. Often she needed to push aside a fear that something could happen to her new father.

Once more Kate dipped the pen into the ink.

> *I love you, Papa.*
> *Your daughter, Kate*

P.S. *I'm glad you married Mama.*

Blotting the ink, Kate folded the page quickly. Tomorrow she'd take the letter to Trade Lake. She'd look—just look—at cloth for Mama.

———

The next morning Anders got up earlier than usual. Putting the harness on Lutfisk, the thirteen-year-old hitched the dog to the sled for hauling wood.

One strap of the harness fit across the dog's chest. Two more straps slipped over his back. At first Anders walked alongside, leading Lutfisk until he grew used to the feel of the sled. Then Anders called out, "Haw!" or "Gee!" Soon Lutfisk learned to turn left or right.

"If you use the same commands, you can help me train him," Anders told Kate as he left for work. "I'm too heavy for Lutfisk to pull, but you're light enough. In a few days you can start putting some of your weight on the sled."

When the sun started to warm the bone-chilling air, Kate put on her skies and set off for Trade Lake. Lutfisk trotted alongside, pulling the sled and learning Kate's commands.

On the far side of Rice Lake, she took off the harness and left the sled near a tree. She didn't want to tire the dog by teaching too much at one time.

When she skied on, Lutfisk followed her to the town of Trade Lake. At Gustafson's Mercantile Store, Kate left her skis in a snowbank. As she started up the steps, she nearly bumped into a man in a black and red mackinaw.

Quickly Kate stepped aside. "Good morning, Mr. Grimm," she said.

The man seemed surprised at her greeting, then smiled politely. His eyes looked like the icy water around which he worked.

"Good morning," he answered. "You're Anders's sister, I believe?"

"Katherine O'Connell," she told him, remembering her brother's description—"Grouch, grouch, all day long."

As Mr. Grimm moved on, Kate wondered if he ever smiled. He seemed just as unhappy as his name. Reaching the top step, Kate turned to see what he was doing.

Just then the man looked back. Meeting Kate's eyes, he spun around and walked quickly away.

Trying to push aside her uneasiness, Kate opened Gustafson's door and walked back to the shelves filled with cloth.

When the clerk showed her the material, Kate found only one piece that would be right for Mama. Kate felt the lovely blue cloth. "Not much left."

"Is it for you?" asked the woman.

"For my mother," Kate told her. "She's going to have a baby."

"And needs a new dress." The clerk smiled. "There's still enough. Just barely, but enough. Shall I wrap it up for you?"

Kate longed to buy the cloth and bring it home to Mama. Yet she had only enough money to mail the letter to Papa.

"I'm sorry," Kate said, and felt her cheeks flush. "But I'll have to wait."

As she turned away from the counter, Kate bumped into a redheaded girl. "Maybelle!" she exclaimed.

"Good morning, Katherine." The other girl sounded as formal as a grown-up. Her voice dripped honey.

"Good morning, Maybelle." Kate answered just as sweetly, but her heart thudded. They hadn't talked together since Kate's birthday.

If Maybelle remembered all that happened that afternoon, she gave no hint of it. Slender and of medium height, she had dark brown eyes and red hair.

Not red, russet, Kate told herself, recalling how Mama corrected her. Kate had never seen such beautiful hair.

Today Maybelle wore curls instead of her usual two braids. As she moved to the counter, her gaze fell on the length of blue cloth.

Kate stopped in the aisle, feeling as though she were going to choke. As she watched to see what happened, Maybelle turned to her.

"My mother told me to buy material for a new dress," Maybelle said. "Do you think this color would be nice with my hair?"

No! Kate wanted to cry, though she knew the cloth would look wonderful. Why did Maybelle ask? Kate doubted that the other girl cared to be friends.

Maybelle took the blue cloth and held it up just beneath her chin. "How does it look?" she wanted to know.

Kate debated with herself. If Maybelle didn't buy the material, it might still be there for Mama.

"I know that when I have such clear, good skin I can wear just about anything," said Maybelle. "And of course my eyes are an asset too. But what do *you* think?"

Kate breathed deep. Mama often told her she mustn't lie. But what if Maybelle bought the cloth?

"It looks very nice," Kate finally croaked, hating herself for telling the truth. Without waiting for an answer, she hurried away. She couldn't bear to see Maybelle buy the lovely cloth.

In the part of the store used as a post office, Kate saw Mr. Fenton get his mail from the postmaster. Moving away from the counter, Mr. Fenton tore open an envelope. As he read the letter, he looked shocked, then angry.

Suddenly he glanced up. Seeing Kate, he smiled. As though a mask had dropped, his face smoothed into pleasant lines.

"Just received some good news from home," he said. Stuffing the letter into its envelope, he headed for the door.

Kate left Papa's letter with the postmaster, then followed Mr. Fenton outside. When the man hurried down the steps, Lutfisk barked.

Ignoring the dog, Mr. Fenton started across the road toward the creamery. But Lutfisk ran after him, continuing to bark.

"Lutfisk!" Kate shouted. "Come here!"

The dog stopped, but bared his teeth and growled.

"Be quiet!" ordered Kate, and Lutfisk obeyed. But not before Mr. Fenton disappeared through the creamery door.

Just then a team of horses and a sleigh turned onto the street. A thin boy with curly blond hair walked alongside, holding the reins.

"Hey, Kate!" he called, and she waved.

Kate had first met Stretch at Spirit Lake School. Even taller than Anders, he was older than the other students. Stretch worked for Mr. Swenson, the father of Kate's friend Josie.

As the horses turned onto a path back of the creamery, Stretch called again. "Wait till I unload this, and I can talk."

When Stretch stopped the horses next to the icehouse, Kate found a place to watch. Through open doors, she saw blocks of ice stacked high, with sawdust around the outer edges of the pile. Mr. Grimm stood on top of the ice, waiting for the tall boy to unload.

Stretch set a wooden ramp with one end on the sleigh, the other end on the top layer of ice. Mr. Grimm slid a pair of large tongs down the ramp. A long rope, tied to one handle of the tongs, passed through the loop of the other handle.

As Stretch set the tongs around a huge block of ice, Mr. Grimm tugged the rope. The tongs tightened. Hand over hand, Mr. Grimm pulled the rope. The tongs and ice followed, sliding up the ramp.

The unloading went quickly. Each time a block of ice started up the ramp, Stretch pushed another large piece into place. Then he waited for the tongs to return to him.

The sleigh was almost empty when a chunk split away from the block at the top of the ramp. The tongs loosened, and the ice broke free. As the block slid down the ramp, it picked up speed.

In the next instant it crashed against Stretch, pinning his hand against another block of ice. Stretch cried out in pain.

"Help!" shouted Kate as she ran forward. Climbing onto the sleigh, she leaned into the block of ice. But she couldn't push it aside.

8

Two Promises

*H*elp!" Kate cried again.

For an instant she stood back. Once again she pushed all her weight into the ice. No matter how hard she tried, the large block would not move.

Stretch groaned. Beads of sweat dotted his forehead.

Then Kate heard a voice behind her. "Get out of the way."

Leaping onto the sleigh, Mr. Grimm tightened tongs around the block of ice. Carefully he pulled it aside, freeing Stretch's hand.

The tall boy dropped to the sleigh. As he cradled his injured hand in his good one, he bit his lip against the pain.

"You need to see a doctor right away," said Mr. Grimm.

"I'll get the buttermaker," Kate said, and slipped away. Soon she returned with Mr. Bloomquist.

Using a clean cloth, the buttermaker wrapped Stretch's hand loosely. Mr. Grimm threw straw into the sleigh to cushion the ride, then covered Stretch with heavy horse blankets.

"I'll take him," said the buttermaker. "Sometimes it's hard to find the doctor. If someone needs me, ask him to wait."

Lifting the reins, Mr. Bloomquist called, "Giddyup!" and urged the horses forward. The team rounded the corner of the creamery and disappeared from sight.

Just then Kate saw Mr. Fenton outside the creamery. With a shrug of his shoulders, he turned away.

Kate trembled. Her knees felt weak, and she sat down on the platform. One moment she felt angry. Didn't Mr. Fenton care about Stretch? He'd been more concerned about his letter than about the accident.

The next moment she wanted to cry, just thinking how Stretch looked. Some of his fingers must have been broken, even crushed. Besides the awful pain now, what would happen to him? Stretch needed strong hands. Josie's father was teaching him to be a blacksmith.

Finally Kate stood up, crossed the street, and put on her skis. Deep in thought, she didn't notice Maybelle until the other girl climbed into a sleigh. But then Kate saw the package under her arm.

The material for Mama's dress! Kate felt sick with disappointment.

As she started home, Lutfisk followed her, jumping up now and then for attention. At Rice Lake Kate again harnessed Lutfisk to the sled. Most of the time he obeyed her commands, and Kate felt good about his progress. But she kept wondering about Mr. Fenton.

What was in the letter he received? Before hiding his feelings, he'd been very upset. *If only I could read that letter*, Kate thought.

By the time she reached Windy Hill Farm, she had decided what she wanted to do. She sought out her mother in the kitchen.

"Mama?" Kate asked as she sat down for cookies and milk.

"Yah, Kate?" Mama's golden blond hair was drawn up, piled on top of her head.

Often Kate felt surprised at how pretty her mother looked. "I've been thinking, Mama."

"Yah?"

"I've been thinking about your little brother Ben."

A flash of pain crossed Mama's face. "I've been thinking too," she said, sitting down next to Kate.

"We can't do anything about Ben," Kate said, stumbling over the words. "I mean, we can pray for him, but we can't do something. Something real, I mean, that we can see."

Mama nodded. "He needs our prayers all right. But what are you trying to say?"

Kate drew a deep breath. She cared so much about this that she was afraid to ask and have Mama say no. Yet she had no choice but to try.

"We can't do anything about Ben," Kate said again. "But we can do something about the person who stole the checks from the creamery."

"Ahhh." Light entered Mama's eyes. "So you're asking me if you can look around even though I already said no."

"Yes, Mama." Kate's voice was small.

Mama stood up, went to the stove, and poured a cup of coffee. When she sat down again, her eyes looked thoughtful. "It would be a way, you say, a way of doing something about Ben. What do you mean?"

"A way of doing something about the kind of thing Ben did," answered Kate softly.

For a time Mama was silent, sipping coffee and staring out the window. "You may be right, Kate," she said at last. "You may be right."

"You mean Anders and I can look around?"

Mama held up her hand. "I have to think about it."

Kate opened her mouth to speak, then closed it again. She couldn't push Mama any further than that.

Just then Lars called.

"Where is he?" Kate asked Mama.

"I moved him into my bedroom," Mama said. "He's starting to cough."

"Oh, Mama!" Kate felt scared. What if the cough developed into pneumonia? Everyone knew there was no good medicine to help.

"I'll sleep on the cot for a while," her mother said. The narrow cot would be uncomfortable for Mama. Yet she could be in the dining room, right next to the bedroom, where she'd hear Lars at night.

So Mama's worried too, Kate thought.

When Kate entered the bedroom, it smelled of onions. Mama had wrapped hot onions in cloth and put them on Lars's chest, hoping to draw out his cough.

Seeing Kate, Lars grinned. But the grin ended in a cough.

"This morning Erik brought over a book," said Kate. "It's named *Call of the Wild*." Books were treasured and passed around from family to family. "Erik said it's about a dog. Want me to read to you?"

Lars nodded. Pulling a chair close to the bed, Kate opened the pages.

> Buck did not read the newspapers, or he would have known that trouble was brewing, not alone for himself, but for every tide-water dog, strong of muscle and with warm, long hair, from Puget Sound to San Diego.

After a time, Kate looked up and saw Lars's eyes closed. She stopped reading, but Lars was listening, not sleeping.

"Kate?" he asked. "Who wrote that book?

"A new author, Jack London."

"I like Buck," Lars told her. "But he was treated so mean."

Kate continued to read. Each time Lars coughed, she listened. The cough sounded loose in his chest, so she felt relieved. Maybe he'd get over this illness faster than the others. When at last he slept, she slipped away.

Putting on her coat, Kate went outside. She'd left the clothes on the line overnight, hoping they'd dry.

Pulling off her mittens, she worked quickly to take in the sheets. Looped over the line, the cloth had frozen together. As Kate tried to separate the edges, the corners tore off in her hands.

Kate sighed and was more careful with the tablecloths. Yet her fingers were clumsy with cold. In spite of her best efforts, the frozen corners again tore.

Taking the basket into the kitchen, Kate hung the sheets over doors to finish drying, then returned to the clothesline. The long one-piece underwear remained. The arms and legs stood out, like people dancing in the wind.

With the arms stretched above her head and the legs doing

an Irish jig, she found the underwear awkward to hold. Growing more tired and cold by the minute, she carried them to the house one by one. As Kate brought in the last pair, Anders looked up from the table.

Her dragging feet caught the threshold. She stumbled, then grabbed the doorjamb. Not for anything would she fall in front of Anders.

Just the same he snickered. "Doing a dance with the underwear?"

Kate stared at him, her anger as hot as an ember in the cookstove. Anders grinned, as if hoping for a fight. But then Kate saw her mother.

Near the cupboard Mama stood with a mixing bowl, her head bowed, her spoon still. Since learning about Ben, she had seemed broken, ready to weep at a moment's notice.

Without speaking, Kate turned her back on Anders and set the table.

When they finished eating supper, Anders stood up, ready to start the chores.

"Sit down," Mama told him. "Kate and I have been talking."

Anders dropped back into his chair.

"I've been thinking about what Kate said," Mama went on. "I've been thinking about my little brother."

Tears came to Mama's eyes, and she brushed them away, as though afraid to show her feelings. "I don't like to see a life wasted."

Her lips trembled as she struggled to speak. "I'm going to give you permission to look for that milk can. If you find the checks or the ledger, you'll help every farmer around Trade Lake."

"Thanks, Mama," said Anders.

In spite of his quiet voice, his eyes filled with excitement. He glanced toward Kate, seeming to ask, "What did you say to her?"

"Just a minute," said Mama. "I'm not done."

She cleared her throat. "You and Kate and Erik are good at solving mysteries. But this is more than just a game. Any person who steals from hardworking farmers has to be a dangerous criminal."

Kate's stomach tightened. Mama had thought about this all right.

"You must promise me something," Mama went on. "You must watch out for each other. Anders, you take care of Kate."

"I will, Mama." Anders flashed his lopsided grin. "I'll take care of my little sister."

"And I'll take good care of my big brother," promised Kate, her voice dangerously sweet. "He always does what I say."

But Mama refused to be sidetracked. "If you find something, you must tell a grown-up at once. You must ask someone like Andrew Anderson number 3 for help."

"We will, Mama," said Anders. For once his voice sounded serious.

Mama looked at Kate.

"I promise, Mama," she said, and meant it. She had no doubt that this was something Mama had carefully considered.

I got what I wanted—Mama's permission, thought Kate. But then she realized what a dangerous request she had made. There might be serious trouble trying to bring such a man to justice.

Deep inside, Kate felt the beginning of fear.

9

The Mysterious Message

I don't want to be afraid, Kate told herself as she had on the day Erik's horses ran away. More than once since then she'd noticed people who seemed to have courage. Now she wondered, *What does it mean to be brave?*

During the evening the outside temperature fell steadily. When Kate went upstairs, strong gusts swooped around the house. Cold seeped through the walls. As she settled into bed, a loud crack rocked the room.

Kate jumped. Her fingers balled into nervous fists as she waited, listening. What was it? A gunshot? What was wrong outside?

Next to her in the bed, Tina slept blissfully on. Kate pulled the quilts over her head and tried to stop trembling. Still the cold stayed with her, as though lodged in her heart.

Anders calls me a scaredy-cat, she thought. *But I won't be afraid.*

In that instant another loud crack shot through the room. Kate tumbled out of bed. Catching up her robe, she raced down the stairs. Feeling her way through the dark, she tiptoed to the dining room. There she lit a candle.

Nearby, Mama lay on the cot. As Kate held up the candle, her mother stirred in her sleep. Kate tiptoed closer, thinking, *She needs to know what's going on.*

When the floorboard creaked, her mother woke with a start. "Kate?" Her sleepy voice seemed to come from far away.

"I'm sorry, Mama. Sorry to wake you."

Her mother yawned. "Is something wrong?"

"A loud noise, Mama. Two loud noises. They sounded like gunshots."

"A gunshot?" Mama sat up, suddenly alert.

Just then the loud crack sounded again. Kate shivered with fear, but her mother laughed.

"Oh, *that!* It's just the house. When the temperature goes way down, the house cracks as it settles."

Kate felt like a small child, afraid over nothing. "I'm sorry I woke you, Mama," she said stiffly.

But her mother took Kate's hand. "I remember the first time I heard that sound. I didn't know what was happening, and it frightened me." Reaching down to the foot of the cot, Mama took a quilt and gave it to Kate. "Why don't you pull up a chair?"

Wrapping herself in the quilt, Kate settled down. As she felt the heat of the wood stove, her embarrassment slipped away.

"Is there anything else that frightens you?" asked Mama.

Kate hesitated. *Should I tell her I'm scared about Papa?* More than once, she'd seen articles in the newspaper. Usually they started with the words "Man hurt in logging camp." Sometimes they even said "Man killed."

"What's wrong?" asked Mama, and Kate felt it safe to begin.

"Could a tree ever fall on Papa?"

"Yah," said Mama. "When lumberjacks cut down the tall pines, the trees sometimes fall the wrong way. And sometimes branches catch in other branches. A tree stays half up and half down. If it falls at a bad time, someone gets hurt."

Kate shivered. "Will Papa be all right?"

"I don't know." Mama was honest. "I hope so."

Kate pulled up her feet, away from the cold floor. "Mama, do you feel scared about Papa?"

"Yah," answered her mother. "Sometimes I'm very scared. I wonder what he's doing—if he's happy, if he's well, if he's been hurt." Mama smiled. "I have a long list. Most of all, I feel scared that he won't come safely home."

Kate clutched the quilt and wrapped herself more tightly. "What do you do? When you're scared, I mean?"

"I pray," said Mama. "I pray for him and all the men. I ask God to help me remember."

"Remember what?" Kate needed to know.

"That no matter what happens, God is with us."

For a long time Kate sat in silence. She felt better just talking about what scared her. "I want to remember too," she said finally.

As Kate crawled back into bed, she heard another loud crack. This time she paid no attention. Her imagination had turned the sounds into gunshots. She didn't want to be tricked again.

I want to know the difference, Kate thought. *I want to know when I need to be afraid, so I'm careful—and when I'm just scared about something that doesn't matter.*

————

On an afternoon when Anders and Erik had time off, the temperature hovered just above freezing. The boys and Kate skied to Little Trade Lake, then on to Big Trade Lake.

The places where ice had been harvested were easy to spot. Sometimes small pine trees marked the corners of a hole. Other times a tangle of branches warned people away from the thin ice.

Whenever Kate and Anders and Erik discovered such a place, they stood at a safe distance from the edge of the hole. Taking turns, they poked around in the water with a long pole. Always they searched for a milk can just beneath the surface. Yet nothing seemed out of the ordinary.

On their way home, they skied into the settlement of Four Corners. There they found Mr. Peters, Kate's organ teacher and choir director at their church.

"You're just the one I want to see," he said to Kate. "I have something to show you."

As they followed him into the church, he told them more. "I want to start a string band."

"A band for playing at church?" Kate asked.

"Certainly," he said. "But it'll be more than that. I'll ask people from other churches too. We'll play for special events around the area."

"We'll travel?" asked Kate. She liked the idea.

"We'll travel." To Mr. Peters it seemed an accomplished fact. "Would you like to play the organ? You'd have no problem with the music. You're coming along well."

Kate felt a warm flush in her cheeks. She knew Mr. Peters didn't pass out compliments unless he meant them. Yet in that moment an ache replaced her excitement. She dreaded what she had to say. "I don't know if I can take lessons anymore." Kate stumbled over the words.

"Because of the stolen cream checks?" Mr. Peters asked. "Don't worry about paying me right now."

But Kate felt torn in two. "If we get behind in the payments, we might not be able to catch up." More than anything else, she wanted to play the organ.

Mr. Peters brushed her concern aside. "Let's just wait and see what happens."

Then Kate thought of something. "How could we take an organ around?"

"I'll show you." Mr. Peters started up a flight of stairs to the balcony and the pipe organ on which Kate took lessons.

Strange, she thought, as she had many times before. *Strange that I should move this close to the first hand-pumped organ in the county*. Often Erik helped Mr. Peters by pushing a wooden handle up and down. The handle worked a bellows, bringing in air to make the pipes sound.

Now the organist walked over to a suitcase sitting on the floor. Picking it up by the handle, he held it out. "Here you are, Kate, a telescope organ. It weighs only thirty-two pounds."

Setting down the oak case, Mr. Peters opened it. To Kate's amazement an organ folded out, complete with pedals, keyboard, and music rack.

Kate giggled. "I can't believe it!"

"Believe it, believe it!" said Anders. Clearly he enjoyed this almost as much as Kate.

Standing in front of the organ, she tried the keys.

"It's like your organ at home," said Mr. Peters. "When you pump the pedals, the air comes in to make the keys sound."

"And you've got music!" Erik exclaimed. He kneeled down and pushed the pedals with his hands.

Kate started to play.

"So, what about it?" asked Mr. Peters.

Kate felt so excited that she laughed. "Of course I want to do it!"

"Good!" said Mr. Peters. "Take the music along, and you can start practicing."

Then he turned to Erik. "Now, what about you? You have a good singing voice. How about an instrument with which you can sing along?"

Erik looked disappointed. "I'd like to play the guitar, but I can't."

In that moment Kate realized how seldom Erik talked about money. Before moving to the farm next to Windy Hill, his father was cheated out of land he owned. As a result, Erik's family found it especially hard to earn the money they needed.

"Tell you what," said Mr. Peters. "I have a guitar you can start out on. I know you'll take good care of it."

A grin lit Erik's face, but Mr. Peters didn't wait for thanks. "Now, Anders, what about you?"

"Me?" Anders looked startled. When Kate laughed, he flushed red.

"Yah certainly, *you*," answered the musician. "What instrument would you like to play?"

Looking nervous, Anders pushed the blond hair out of his eyes.

To Kate's amazement, he seemed at a loss for words. "I'll think about it," he said at last.

Kate blinked. Was Anders really willing to play an instrument? He never seemed interested in music.

"You let me know," Mr. Peters answered. "If we work hard,

we'll play in Central Park on Fourth of July and Midsummer Day."

When they left the church, Kate felt that she skied on clouds instead of a snowy road. *Maybe I'll really become a great organist,* she thought. *I'll be like Jenny Lind. I'll encourage people with my music. I'll help them feel better.*

"Well, Kate, it's a start," Erik said, and she knew he was happy for her.

But Anders smirked. "Can you see my little sister? Traveling around Burnett County, playing the organ?"

He turned to Erik. "Do you remember whose company we have the pleasure of keeping?"

Erik grinned, and Anders went on. "You may think this is my little sister." With a flourish of his hand he pointed toward Kate. "But this truly is a woman of great musical gifts."

An angry flush warmed Kate's cheeks. "Aw, Anders, be quiet!" Somehow he always made her dream sound ridiculous.

"What?" he asked. "Would you tell me not to speak? Some-day—*someday,* mind you, I will travel around the country, yea, around the world. I will travel ahead of you, putting up posters, advertising your coming. 'Miss Katherine O'Connell,' they will say. 'Come to hear this accomplished organist. She plays like Miss Jenny Lind sings.' "

When Erik hid a grin, Kate felt even more angry. "Stop it!" she said to Anders. "Stop it, stop it, stop it!"

But with Anders there was no stopping. "Oh ho! Methinks the lady is angry." His voice turned serious. "Kate, my dear, you must learn how to act when you go on stage."

But Kate stuck out her tongue at him. The moment she did, she felt embarrassed. *I'm thirteen years old! Almost grown-up!* As tears welled into her eyes, she skied off, unwilling to let Anders or Erik see her cry.

But her brother's voice followed her. "I'll tell everyone you're my sister. I'll say, 'I knew her when—' "

Blinking away tears, Kate turned back. "And I'll say, 'I'm not related to you!' "

Once again she took off and was still ahead when they reached the bridge over Trade River. In spite of his longer legs,

Anders skied more slowly, still careful of the ankle he'd sprained.

But Erik called ahead. "Let's stop at the creamery and find out how Stretch is doing."

They found Josie Swenson's father talking to the buttermaker. Mr. Swenson looked upset, and Kate remembered how much he wanted to help Stretch.

"Doc Jonas doesn't like it," Mr. Swenson said. "Two of Stretch's fingers are badly smashed. Doc told me to take Stretch to Minneapolis. We'll go tomorrow and see what another doctor can do."

Mr. Swenson shook his head. "Stretch needs that hand if he's going to be a blacksmith. He can't get a good grip on the sledge without it."

As though it were yesterday, Kate remembered Stretch's dream. He wanted to make good. He'd even said, "I'd like my own shop someday. Maybe in Grantsburg." Would Stretch lose his dream because of one block of ice?

Kate looked down at her own fingers. She knew how much she needed them to play the organ.

"Matilda is going with us," said Mr. Swenson, talking about his wife. "We'll take all of the children except Josie. She'll take care of the animals."

He looked at Kate. "Will you help with the milking and keep her company overnight?"

Kate grinned. "I'd like to. Tell Josie I'll come over tomorrow afternoon. Before dark."

When Mr. Swenson left, Anders asked the buttermaker, "Has anything more come up?

Mr. Bloomquist shook his head. "Not about the stolen money." But Kate had the feeling he wasn't telling everything.

––––––––––

That night Kate jumped out of bed twice, thinking she heard a noise outside her window. Each time, she saw a sleigh pass the house, using the shortcut through the woods to Spirit Lake.

Toward morning Kate decided what to do about a dress for Mama. When she woke again, it was daylight. Tina had slipped out of bed to dress downstairs by the stove. As Kate pulled the quilts off her head, she saw her breath in the frosty air. A draft seeped through the windows and outside walls. Before long, Kate's nose felt icy.

Bounding out of bed, she dressed quickly. Her fingers fumbled in the cold. In her warm dress and wool sweater and stockings, she hurried to a window. As she looked off in the distance, the snow glistened, white and beautiful.

Then Kate looked down, close to the house. In the snowbank on the other side of the track, there seemed to be letters—large letters that spelled words.

Kate's heart pounded as she read the warning:

STOP SNOOPING

10

The Vanishing Footprints

Stop snooping?

In spite of the cold room, Kate stood at the window looking down. Sure enough, in the bank of snow across the track, the letters stood out. She wasn't imagining the words.

Even worse, Kate realized what the message meant. *Someone was here last night. Right outside our house.*

Kate began to shake, whether from cold or fear, she wasn't sure. Yet she felt certain of one thing. Mama didn't need to see this message. Not right now. Not with Papa gone and the baby coming.

Running to the door of her bedroom, Kate called out, "Anders!"

When he didn't answer, she hurried down the stairs. Where was he, anyway? Out in the barn? Then he, too, had seen the message.

She found Anders sitting in the kitchen, calmly eating his breakfast.

As Anders looked at Kate, he seemed to read her face. Stuffing half a piece of bread in his mouth at once, he stood up. "Well, better get to the chores."

Kate pulled on her coat and went outside. Anders followed. Kate headed toward the trail that led through the farm.

"What's wrong?" asked Anders.

"C'mon. I'll show you." Kate marched straight to the bank of snow, then stopped. "What do you see?"

"S-T-O—" Here on the ground Anders needed to step back. "Stop snooping?"

Kate watched him, her eyes wide.

"Oh, Kate, it's a joke!"

"A *joke?*"

"Sure, one of the boys from school. Someone came through last night—" Anders stopped in midsentence. "Last night. After we spent all day looking around." He stepped forward and stared at the letters. "I guess you're right, Kate. It's not a joke."

"But who would do a such a thing?" she asked. "Creeping in here during the middle of night. Standing outside our windows, writing in the snow."

"Pretty awful." Anders looked angry.

Kate felt the same way. "At first it scared me. Now it makes me mad. Who does that person think he is, coming onto our farm and *threatening* us?"

"*He?* We don't know it's a he."

Kate sighed. "No, I guess we don't. But if it's the person who carried the milk can and rock, it has to be someone strong."

"Guess you're right," Anders said, clearly not liking the idea. "It's probably a man." Grinning, he flexed his muscles. "Or a big strong boy."

Once again they studied the letters in the snowbank.

"Whoever it was used a long pole," said Anders. "He stood on the trail and reached over."

"A long pole?" Kate was thinking. "Like the kind used to push ice around?"

"Could be," said Anders, "though I suppose he could use the handle of a rake or shovel." As he stood on the trail, he reached out, judging how far his hand would extend.

"Nope. It would have to be a pole—the kind you're talking

about, the kind used for harvesting ice."

"So maybe it's someone you work with."

"Yup," said Anders. "But it wouldn't have to be. Every family that takes in ice has one of those poles."

Once again Kate stared at the words. This time she saw something she hadn't noticed before. "Look!" she exclaimed, pointing.

On the left side of the message, between the trail on which they stood and the first S, was one boot print.

"Only one," said Anders.

"As though he wanted to leave it there," added Kate.

Anders studied the print. "I think you're right. It doesn't look as though he lost his balance and stepped forward by mistake."

"It's like a signature. Like someone saying, 'This is me. Watch out.' " Kate started shaking again.

"Ah, come on, Scaredy-cat!" Anders said when he saw her tremble. "We're not going to let him get the best of us."

Kate's teeth chattered, but she tightened her fists. Trying to hide her shaking, she leaned down to look at the boot print. Suddenly she noticed something. Her shivering stopped.

"Anders!"

"Ah, the lady made a discovery!"

"Be serious!" said Kate. "It's the footprint we followed through the woods that night."

"Yah, sure, you betcha." Anders shook his head and his blond hair fell into his eyes. "That's the boot print for a four-buckle overshoe. Every man and boy in Burnett County has a pair of boots like that."

Kate felt disappointed. "Well, how about the size?"

Again Anders shook his head. "About medium size. Not real big, not real little. In fact, *my* boots are bigger than his."

Kate grinned. "But you have awfully big feet!" Then she realized something. "At least we know that print isn't yours. Let's look around. Maybe there's more boot prints that size."

They started by searching the trail that passed through the farmyard, then dropped down the steep hill into the woods.

Soon Kate and Anders realized their search was hopeless. Sleighs and horses, using the shortcut to Spirit Lake, had crisscrossed the snow. There was no way to tell what direction the man took.

"Well, there's one thing we *can* do," said Kate. "Let's wipe out the words."

Anders started back to the snowbank. "I want Erik to see them."

"He'll be coming soon to pick you up. But we need to figure out how to get hold of him—when Erik doesn't know we need him, I mean."

Anders snorted. "Stop talking nonsense."

"That's not nonsense. There must be some way we can send messages back and forth."

"Well, we can't signal with a mirror," Anders said. "That'd be all right if there were just a field between us. But there's also a big woods."

Just the same, he had a think-it-through look in his eyes. Kate felt sure his mind was ticking faster than a clock.

A moment later, Lutfisk bounded up. Pulling off his mittens, Anders knelt down to scratch behind the dog's ears. Lutfisk stretched out his long tongue and licked his master's face.

Anders grinned. "I know what we can do! Lutfisk gets the cows when I tell him. Why can't we train him to get Erik?"

"Why not?" Kate liked the idea. "I'll sew a little cloth bag. You can tie it to a rope and put the rope around Lutfisk's neck."

"Yup, that would do it!" Anders looked as excited as Kate felt.

Getting his ski pole, he walked into the bank of snow. "I'm not going to wait for Erik." Carefully he wiped out every letter. "Mama doesn't need something more to worry about."

"But we have to tell Mr. Bloomquist," said Kate.

"Or Andrew Anderson number 3." Anders started for the barn.

For a minute Kate stood there, looking off over Rice Lake. In the morning sunlight the surrounding hills seemed quiet, peaceful, safe.

But then Anders called to her. "C'mere, Kate!"

When she came near to the barn, Anders held up his hand, stopping her. "Look!" He pointed down.

In front of the door the tracks of people and animals mingled. But in the snow just off the path, Kate saw one medium-sized boot print. "It's not yours, is it?" Even as she asked, she knew the answer.

"Like you said, my feet are bigger."

"I don't think he meant for us to see this one," said Kate slowly.

Anders agreed. "If he came in the dark, he probably didn't know he stepped off the path."

Then Kate had an even worse thought. "You know what, Anders? That boot print points right toward the barn, as though someone opened the door and walked in. Whoever wrote the message could still be hiding in there."

Anders scowled. "Thanks a lot! Can't you think of something better to tell me?" Watching where he stepped, he looked for more medium-sized boot prints.

Inside the fence that extended beyond one end of the barn, the cows and sheep had trampled the snow, hiding any possible evidence. Anders and Kate turned away from there, knowing any search was hopeless.

The trail to Spirit Lake passed close to the other end of the barn. Staring at the tracks, Anders shook his head.

Kate saw what he meant. Here, too, sleighs and horses had crisscrossed the snow.

"Well, better get it over with." Anders returned to the side door of the barn. Slowly he pushed it open. In the stillness the door creaked loudly.

Anders waited, as though listening, then peered into the gloomy shadows.

Close at hand, two cows turned their heads to watch. From farther away, Wildfire whinnied her greeting. Beyond that, the sheep softly bleated.

Kate followed Anders inside. In the half light her brother seized a pitchfork and stalked from one end of the barn to the other.

11

Sounds From the Darkness

Two cats leaped out from behind a barrel. Kate jumped. But Anders walked on, searching the shadows.

Still holding the pitchfork, he climbed the ladder to the loft. As he crossed from one end of the haymow to the other, the floorboards creaked. From overhead his footsteps sounded as heavy as a man's.

Finally Anders started throwing hay down through the hole onto the main floor. Kate spread it out for Wildfire and the cows, but she felt uneasy. Someone could easily hide in the great mound of hay in the loft. Without moving all that hay, it would be impossible to find him.

As Anders milked the cows, Kate went to the hen house. Finding the water frozen, she brought warm water from the house. As she fed the chickens, she kept a wary eye on Big Red.

When Tina came in, the rooster looked up from the morsel he pecked. Cocking his head, he cast a beady eye toward Tina, then started toward her.

Backing away, Tina held out her hands to ward him off. But

Kate took no chances. Bounding over, she stood in front of the little girl.

As though to say "Who do you think you are?" the rooster stretched back his long neck. Flapping his wings, he flew upward. As his claw reached out, the sharp spur on his leg tore Kate's skin.

"Owwwww!" she cried, jumping out of reach. "Ow, ow, ow!"

At a safe distance, Kate checked her leg. Her wool stocking was torn as well as her long underwear. Drops of blood left red stains.

When Mama saw Kate's leg, she exclaimed, "That rooster!" Soon after, she told Anders, "I want you to butcher that old chicken. He's too mean and tough for frying, but we'll have a good stew."

As the family finished breakfast, bells jingled in the yard. Kate pulled on her warm coat. "I want to ride with Erik and Anders to Trade Lake," she told Mama. "I'll ski back." Clutching a package, she hurried outside.

Anders loaded their milk cans into the sleigh. Kate put in her skis, then climbed up between Erik and her brother. On the way to town, she and Anders told Erik about the message in the snow.

"And guess what?" said Kate. "Anders is going to train Lutfisk to fetch you!"

Erik grinned. "*Fetch* me?"

"Like he does the cows!" Kate enjoyed the joke. "We'll tie a little cloth bag around his neck. If Lutfisk obeys, we can get hold of you whenever we want."

"Good idea!" Erik said. "Let's start training him after work this afternoon. He won't have trouble learning."

At the creamery Erik and Anders unloaded their milk cans. "Can we talk for a minute?" Anders asked the buttermaker.

Mr. Bloomquist led the three of them from the large room into the small one and closed the door between. As they sat down, Andrew Anderson came in through the door leading directly outside. Anders told the two men about the message and the boot prints.

I don't like it!" exclaimed Mr. Anderson. "Your father's gone, and you folks are alone on the farm."

"Is there anything more we need to know?" asked Anders. "Anything that would help us figure out who the man could be?"

The buttermaker looked at Mr. Anderson. When the older man nodded, Mr. Bloomquist spoke quietly. "Andrew and I didn't want to get you any more involved. But in spite of our good plans, you're in the middle of this. You might as well know we aren't getting our checks from New York."

"What do you mean?" asked Kate.

"Every Wednesday the creameries in this area haul tubs of butter to Grantsburg. We fill up a refrigerated railroad car. It reaches New York in time for the Monday morning market."

"They like our product," said Mr. Anderson. "Burnett County butter always brings a cent above market price. But we aren't getting paid. For three weeks we haven't received a check."

Anders turned to Kate. "Do you understand what that means?"

"I think so. The farmers bring in their milk. The creamery separates it and keeps the cream that makes the butter. The creamery sends the butter to New York. And if New York doesn't pay, the farmers don't get paid. Right?"

"You've got it." The scowl was back on her brother's face.

"It affects all the farmers who bring in cream," said Mr. Anderson. "Which is just about every farmer in the Trade Lake area."

Kate sighed. "It's getting worse all the time, isn't it?"

"But there's something to give us hope." Mr. Anderson squared his shoulders. "The bank gave us a short-term loan to help until checks come from New York. We'll reissue the checks for the farmers."

"Write them out again?" Kate asked. "I thought you couldn't because the ledger was stolen."

"It was. But we still have some daily work sheets. Our good buttermaker used them to record how much cream each farmer brought in. For some strange reason, some are missing. But we'll do what we can."

"You'll add up those amounts?" asked Erik.

Mr. Anderson nodded. "We can't pay the full amount until

we find the ledger. But we'll make out checks for what we know. It'll take time, but we can do it."

Time, thought Kate. *Just what we don't have. Mama needs a new dress now.*

"If all goes well," said Anders.

"If all goes well." Mr. Anderson sighed.

Watching his eyes, Kate wondered, *How long will a bank loan money to a business where everything is going wrong?* The bank had a responsibility to other customers too.

"I have to go to North Branch for a few days," Mr. Anderson continued. "I need a better hiding place for the work sheets."

Anders looked at Kate and grinned. "Well, we know just the place."

Kate laughed. "Why don't you take them over to Swensons' right away, before Mr. Swenson leaves? Tell him Kate and Anders and Erik sent you."

Soon after, Mr. Anderson left by the door leading directly outside. Anders and Erik followed. Through the window, Kate saw them turn the horses toward the ice harvesting on Little Trade Lake.

Using the other door, Kate walked into the main room. Already Mr. Bloomquist was taking milk from a farmer. Stopping in front of the large wooden churn, Kate watched it rotate.

Then she heard low voices. Curious, Kate walked around to the other side of the churn and found Gunnar Grimm and LeRoy Fenton. As she stared at the men, they stopped talking.

Kate's heart pounded. *There're so many doors in this place. How long have they been here?*

She wished she could run from the room. Instead, she walked slowly toward the outside door, trying to pretend it wasn't important that she saw them. As she crossed the street, her mind raced. *Gunnar Grimm. LeRoy Fenton. What did it mean?*

The morning felt warm for January, and Kate welcomed the gentle breeze. At least there was one thing she could do. Clutching the package she'd brought from home, she hurried into Gustafson's store. When the clerk showed her the material she had on hand, Kate's heart sank. There was nothing as nice as that blue cloth.

"Sorry," she said finally. "I just don't see what I want."

"Is it for yourself?" the woman asked.

Kate shook her head. "For my mother."

"Ahhh!" The clerk remembered. "You're Kate O'Connell. Your mother's going to have a baby."

Feeling miserable, Kate nodded. If only she'd been able to buy the material the other day, before Maybelle came in. Now it was too late.

But the clerk folded back a large piece of cloth. "Here it is—under here. Isn't this what you wanted?"

In the dim light of the store the blue cloth seemed alive with color. "It's still here?" Kate couldn't believe it.

The clerk smiled. "Yah."

"But Maybelle was going to buy that piece!"

The clerk looked as though she wanted to laugh. "Maybelle purchased green material instead. She told me, 'If Kate says the color looks wonderful, it must be awful.' "

Kate giggled. "And I was telling the truth!"

She set down the package she'd brought along. As she opened the wrapping, she gazed at the mittens and long scarf inside. Hand knit and warm, they were also beautiful. Mama had knitted them as a Christmas gift, using more expensive red yarn.

As Kate touched the wool, her hand lingered, feeling the softness. She had worn the scarf and mittens only once.

Tempted to change her mind, she spoke quickly. "Can I trade these for the blue cloth?"

"Trade the scarf and mittens? They're lovely," said the clerk. "And they're unusually well made." She seemed to guess how much Mama's gift meant to Kate. "Are you sure you want to give them up?"

For a moment Kate hesitated. "Yes," she said finally. "You make trades, don't you?"

"Yah." The clerk still looked unwilling. "If you're sure. And you can pick out some lace for your mother's dress."

Kate thought quickly. If Mama wanted lace, she could take some from another dress. "Can I get a small piece of flannel instead?"

The woman smiled. "A small piece."

As soon as the clerk wrapped the material, Kate hurried from the store. All the way to Windy Hill Farm she thought about what she'd done. One moment she felt excited. The next moment she remembered the red scarf and mittens.

When Kate reached home, she led Mama to her favorite chair. "Sit down," Kate said. "Close your eyes. Open your hands!" She placed the package on her mother's outstretched palms.

Mama pulled aside the paper wrapping and gasped, "Oh, Kate!" Carefully she stroked the blue material. "How did you buy such lovely cloth?" As she heard the story, tears welled up in her eyes.

Then, from beneath the dress material, Kate pulled the flannel cloth. "For the baby," she said. Seeing Mama's soft smile, Kate felt glad she'd made the trade.

Late that afternoon she skied to Josie's. Kate looked forward to being with her friend. They'd talk half the night together.

Bounding alongside, Lutfisk yipped and jumped in Kate's way. Finally he sniffed some rabbit tracks and bounded off.

As the winter sun set in the west, Kate and Josie brought in Swensons' cows and milked them. By the time they finished, night had settled over the farm.

The main floor of Swensons' log house had two rooms—a sitting and eating area and a large kitchen. Between the two rooms, stairs went up to the second floor.

"Can you imagine all my brothers on that train?" asked Josie as she and Kate ate supper at the kitchen table.

Kate laughed. Her friend had six brothers and two sisters. "Jacob and Joshua, Jonah and Jesse, Jethro and James. And Rebecca and Jennifer."

Finally Kate had gotten them all straight, even remembering their names. But she had to say them in order like a rhyme.

Across the table, Josie leaned forward. "I've got so much to tell you!" With no school until April 8, they didn't get to see each other as often as they liked.

Just then Kate heard something—a strange sound that seemed to come from along the outside wall. "What was that?" she asked, looking toward the large window next to the table.

"What was what?" Josie answered. "I didn't hear anything." Kate went back to eating. A moment later she heard a scratching noise, as though something were dragged along the wall.

Standing up, Kate went to the window and peered out. She saw nothing but the blackness of night.

Slowly Kate sat down. She was positive she'd heard a noise. But the glass pane yawned dark and cold and empty. "Is there some way to cover that window?" she asked.

"Why?" Josie looked as though she thought her friend a bit strange. "There's nothing out there."

"How do you know?"

"I just know," said Josie.

But Kate had lived in Minneapolis. She didn't like having windows without shades pulled at night.

"Stop acting like a city girl," Josie told her. "Out in the country there's never anyone around."

Kate settled back in her chair, unwilling to show her friend how uneasy she felt.

"Now, tell me everything that's happened," said Josie. Her soft skin seemed to glow in the light of the kerosene lamp.

But Kate once more heard the noise. Wanting more light, she said, "I can hardly see to eat. Do you have another lamp?"

Josie laughed. "Anders is right. You *are* a scaredy-cat! And you're supposed to keep *me* company!"

Kate swallowed. Even so, she carried a lamp from the other room into the kitchen. Carefully she set the lamp on the end of the table closest to the window.

Just then the scratching started again, louder this time. "Oh!" said Josie, her hazel eyes widening with fright. "Now I know what you mean."

"Any ideas?" asked Kate, trying to sound calm and unafraid.

Josie shook her head. "It can't be a branch rubbing against the house. There's no tree there."

"Then what *is* it?" asked Kate.

"I don't know," Josie whispered. "What should we do?"

"Maybe we could take a quilt," Kate whispered back. "We could hang it over the window. If there's someone there, he couldn't see us."

"*He*? Who do you think it is?" Josie's eyes looked as round as silver dollars.

"I don't know, but whoever it is couldn't see us."

Josie nodded, too scared to speak.

Kate looked toward the window. "Is there some way I could fasten a quilt at the top?"

But just then a head appeared above the windowsill—a head with beady black eyes.

In terror Kate pushed back her chair. It fell over, crashing against the floor.

12

The Secret Room

*J*osie!" Kate cried.

Her friend was already hiding under the kitchen table. "Come down here," Josie whispered, her voice hoarse.

But Kate felt too frightened to move. She stared at the darkened window.

As she watched, the head moved closer, closer. Yes, the eyes were large and beady. Something red waved above them.

Kate clutched the edge of the kitchen table. Now a large yellow beak appeared. The mouth opened and closed. Through the glass Kate heard a hoarse cry. *Cock-a-doodle-doooooo!*

Suddenly Kate started to laugh. She dropped into a chair.

"Are you crazy?" asked Josie from under the table.

Kate held her sides with laughter. "Cock-a-doodle-dooo, all right!"

When Kate could stand up, she flung open the kitchen door. Hurrying around the corner, she grabbed Anders as he and Erik tried to get away.

"You boys!" sputtered Kate. "How can you do such an awful thing? Scaring Josie out of her wits!"

Anders snorted. "Scaring Kate, you mean. Not a bad joke, huh?"

"I'll get even with you!" Kate stormed.

But her brother's hand darted out, thrusting the rooster's head in her face.

Backing away, Kate ran up the steps. When she reached the doorway, she turned. "Well, as long as you're here, you might as well come in. Josie's got cookies."

"What a gracious invitation!" Anders exclaimed. Just the same, he and Erik started for the house.

By the time they reached the kitchen, Josie was out from under the table. Smoothing her hair, she smiled at Anders.

Taking off his cap, he pushed back his thatch of blond hair. A lopsided grin lit his face. Anders had more than one reason for walking this far, Kate felt sure.

She glanced at Erik. *Does he feel the same way about me?*

As her fear disappeared, Kate's normal curiosity returned. "How did you *do* that?" she asked Anders. She recognized Big Red's head. The rooster must have found his way into the stew pot. "How do you make his beak open and close?"

Anders laughed. "Kate, your curiosity is going to get the best of you someday."

Erik explained. "See this muscle in the rooster's neck?" Anders pulled it up and down.

Kate still didn't want to get too close.

After devouring Josie's cookies, Anders told Kate, "I discovered more footprints."

Her eyes widened. "Where?"

"On the one side of the barn we didn't check. You know that back door? I found footsteps leading away."

"And you followed them?"

"Not very far. A short way off they disappeared. Vanished. Blotted out by blowing snow."

When the boys left for home, Josie told Kate to bring a lamp. "I want to show you something."

Josie led her to the secret room they'd discovered a short time before. Kate hadn't seen the room since the day they found it. She felt eager to look around.

Together they opened the door, then stepped inside. The room was narrow, probably three feet wide at most, but also long. On one end, the ceiling was high enough for a man to stand. On the other end, the ceiling went close to the floor.

As Kate set the lamp down, Josie picked up a carefully wrapped package.

"What is it?" asked Kate.

"Before Papa left, Andrew Anderson number 3 came over. He told Papa that you and Anders sent him."

Kate grinned. "We sent him all right."

"Papa said, 'I'm going to Minneapolis today.' They talked about it. Finally they agreed on something. When Papa left, he told me, 'I put some papers in the secret room. They'll be safe there. No one knows we have them.' "

So Mr. Anderson had liked their idea! Kate felt glad. Certainly the hidden room had to be the safest place around. Leaving the package in a corner of the room, Kate and Josie returned to the kitchen.

As they cleaned up supper dishes, Kate heard a sound along the road. "What's that?" she asked, and listened again.

She couldn't decide what she heard. Perhaps a horse coming their way. Yet there was something strange. Was the horse moving slowly, as though the driver didn't want anyone to know?

Kate blew out the nearest kerosene lamp. "Josie, get the other one."

As the second flame flickered out, the girls stood in darkness. "What's wrong?" Josie whispered.

"I think there's a horse coming. But if there is, it's not wearing bells."

"But everyone puts bells on their harness," answered Josie.

"I know," Kate whispered. "Shhh!"

Together they crept into the large open room. Standing well back, they gazed out the window.

The night was too dark for Kate and Josie to see well, but the outline of a horse seemed to pass between the sky and the house.

Kate ducked down. "It's the boys," she whispered as a horse and cutter stopped at the hitching rail. "They've got Wildfire this time. They're coming back to scare us."

As the girls watched, something shadowy moved next to the

horse. Kate heard the clink of harness. "It's Anders and Erik all right. How can we scare *them*?"

Moving away from Kate, Josie crawled forward to one side of the window. Even as she peered out, she edged back. "Kate, it's—"

But Kate interrupted. "How can we get even?"

On her hands and knees, she crawled closer to the other side of the window. Trying to stay out of sight, she stared into the darkness.

"Kate—" Josie started again.

Just then the person turned away from his horse. For a moment his heavyset body seemed outlined against the snow. In that instant Kate felt panic in every part of her being.

She scrambled back from the window. "Josie—" In the darkness Kate's voice trembled.

"I know," answered her friend. "It's not the boys. What can we do?"

As she spoke, a boot squeaked on the snowy path leading to the house.

Kate had only one moment to think. Staying on her hands and knees, she crawled toward the secret room. Finding the latch, she opened the door, and slipped inside. Josie followed close behind.

With no windows, the small room was even darker than the one they left. But Kate closed the door behind them.

"Kate—" said Josie.

Laying a hand on her friend's arm, Kate whispered, "Shhh! There's someone at the outside door."

"I wish we could see," Josie whispered back.

The two girls strained to hear. The door into the house creaked. Next to the floor, Kate felt a rush of cold air. The door closed.

Kate and Josie sat without moving, scarcely breathing. From their hiding place, they heard the scratch of a match.

Kate seemed to see a small, flickering light. Then it disappeared. Had she imagined it?

Again she heard a match being lit. From her place next to the door, she gazed up. Above her head, she saw a dim light. As she watched, the light brightened. Had the intruder lit a kerosene lamp?

In the next moment Kate realized something. *If light can come in, I can see out*. Without making a sound, she stood up.

Moving her fingers toward the splinter of light, Kate found small pieces of wood set into the door. Like narrow slats, they slid beneath her hand. One moved up, another down, leaving a crack wide enough to look through.

Kate moved her face closer to the crack. Someone stood at the dining room table, holding the lamp. A cap covered his hair, and his back was turned toward Kate.

A man of medium height—strong, muscular, and wearing a red and black plaid mackinaw. Who was he? LeRoy Fenton and Gunnar Grimm both had such jackets.

Kate watched each movement. *Look this way!* she wanted to cry.

Instead, the man moved toward the opposite wall. Holding out the lamp, he started around the room, knocking the wall with his free hand. Why was he here?

In that moment Kate remembered the two men listening in the creamery. Was this one of them? Was he trying to find the daily work sheets?

As the man passed to the other side of the wood stove, Kate lost sight of him. From the sound of his movements, she decided that he had started around the end wall.

Where's Lutfisk? Kate wondered. If ever she needed him, it was now! But she heard no bark, no dog somewhere in the woods, chasing rabbits. Not even off in the distance.

Instead, she felt a movement. Close to her feet, Josie quietly shifted her position in the darkness.

Right outside the hidden room, the heavy footsteps moved toward them. Closer and closer the man came. *Why is he searching?* Kate wondered again.

Near at hand he rapped the wall, and Kate had a terrible thought. *Maybe he's looking for me*.

Heart in her throat, she stepped back. Suddenly she felt something beneath her foot.

Josie gasped.

I stepped on her hand! Kate thought.

The man drew closer, still rapping. Would the door sound hollow? What if he discovered the peephole Kate used?

With all her heart, she wanted to look out, to see the face of the man who searched. With all her heart, she knew she could not. If she stepped on Josie again, her friend might cry out.

13

More Bad News

$\mathcal{T}$hen the man rapped, directly in front of Kate, but above the slats and below. After what seemed hours, he walked on.

Careful of Josie this time, Kate moved forward. As she peered through the narrow crack, the light moved out of the room.

For a minute Kate waited, wanting to be sure. Finally she knelt down next to Josie. "He's in the kitchen."

Josie breathed deeply, as though she'd held her breath all that time. As they listened to the man move around, neither of the girls spoke.

When Kate once again stood up, she saw a sliver of light near the doorway. Instead of entering the room, the unwelcome visitor started up the stairs. Step by heavy step, he climbed to the second floor.

"What do you think he's looking for?" asked Josie.

"For the papers, don't you think?" At least that's what Kate wanted to believe.

"Mr. Anderson's papers?" Josie sounded disturbed. "But no one knows they're here."

"*Someone* knows he brought them," Kate whispered. "That someone is in this house!"

Just then the heavy footsteps started down the stairs. Kate took her place at the peek hole, trying for a glimpse of the intruder's face.

Yet when the man came into her line of vision, she saw only his back. Setting the lamp on the table, he blew out the flame.

As Kate's eyes adjusted to the darkness, she felt rather than saw the man move to the outside door. When it creaked, she knew it opened. When it creaked again, she believed it closed. But was the intruder inside or out?

Without moving, Kate and Josie waited in the secret room. Her ear close to the slats, Kate heard hooves along the icy road. At first near at hand, they gradually moved off in the distance. Finally the hoofbeats stopped. Only then did the girls come out of their hiding place.

"We should look outside," said Kate. "Maybe the man left footprints."

"Maybe," said Josie. "But you're not going to catch me out in the dark. I'm staying right here."

Kate started for the door, but Josie called her back. "Kate, we're here all alone. There's no one else around."

Kate pulled on her coat.

"What if that awful man left his horses and walked back?" Josie asked. "You wouldn't hear him."

Her hand on the doorknob, Kate stopped. She didn't like the idea of going out in the dark any more than Josie. "I'll look in the morning," Kate said, slowly taking off her coat. "It's not snowing. If there are tracks, they'll still be there."

From that time on they lit no lamps. Instead, they pulled quilts from Josie's bed and spread them out on the floor of the secret room. Long after they crawled between the blankets, they lay awake in the darkness.

"I'm scared," said Josie at last.

"Me too," answered Kate. They had taken off their shoes, but still wore their dresses.

"Do you think he'll come back?" Josie's voice quavered.

"No, I don't think so." Kate wanted to be strong for her friend. Instead, she felt shivers of fear.

The secret room was getting cold. Kate opened the door a

crack to let in heat from the nearby stove. As she tried to settle down, she thought about the night their house made loud cracking sounds.

"What do you do when you're scared?" she had asked.

"I pray," Mama had said. "And I ask God to help me remember."

"Remember what?" Kate wanted to know.

"That no matter what happens, God is with us."

I want to remember too, Kate thought now, as she had on that night. Soon she fell asleep, warm and tucked away as if in a nest, within the secret room.

————

The next morning Kate woke to the barking of a dog. "Where am I?" she muttered as she opened her eyes. The room was dark with only a sliver of light.

As she came fully awake, she thought back to the evening before. The boys coming to scare them. The man who entered the house, searching for something. The hidden room that sheltered them.

The dog continued barking, as though trying to get their attention. Sometimes he seemed close at hand, other times farther away. But the bark seemed familiar.

"Lutfisk!" Kate exclaimed. "What's he doing here?"

Scrambling out from beneath the quilts, she slipped on her shoes and hurried to a window in the large open room. It was Lutfisk all right. He bounded between Swensons' front door and the hitching rail.

As Kate stepped outside, the dog's bark changed to a joyful yelp. His tail wagging, he raced up the steps onto the porch.

Kate knelt down and hugged the dog. When he licked her face, she drew back and laughed. "Good boy!" she exclaimed, relieved to have him here. "Where were you last night when I needed you?"

Lutfisk barked, a quick, short yip, as though talking to her.

"I suppose you want your ears scratched," said Kate. Lutfisk wiggled and yipped again.

In the bright morning light the snow twinkled, as though

covered with diamonds. In such a world Kate's fear of the night before seemed impossible. Had someone really entered Swensons' house?

Recalling her plan to look for footprints, Kate stood up. Usually the Swenson family used the kitchen door. Maybe the unwelcome visitor made the only tracks to the front door.

Walking to the edge of the porch, Kate looked down. She groaned, feeling sick all the way through. "Why did I wait?"

She found it hard to remember how afraid she'd been. "Why didn't I look right away?" She only blamed herself.

Lutfisk bounded off the steps. Kate tried to catch him, but it was already too late. For some time the dog had run back and forth between the porch and hitching rail. Any human footprints were covered by those of Lutfisk.

Walking up and down the path, Kate searched, but finally had to give up. Not one clear boot print remained.

———————

When Kate left Josie's, she skied to Trade Lake. She found Anders and Erik on their lunch hour, warming up in the creamery.

Just seeing them, Kate felt better. Sitting down in the room with the steam boiler, she spoke in a low voice, telling the boys what had happened last night.

"You never saw the man's face?" Anders asked.

Kate shook her head. "But he looked strong. Medium height, shorter than you. He wore a red and black plaid mackinaw."

Her brother snorted. "You're describing half the men in Burnett County. Did you see his hair?"

Again Kate had to say no. "Covered up by a cap."

Erik scowled. "I don't like it. You and Josie were there alone!"

Anders felt the same way. "What if that man found you? We better tell the buttermaker."

They found Mr. Bloomquist in the large open room, packing butter into sixty-pound tubs. With quick movements, he placed a circle of parchment in the bottom of a tub, then another piece of parchment around the sides.

"We need to talk to you," Anders said.

"Bad news?" the buttermaker asked, his voice low.

Anders nodded.

Mr. Bloomquist glanced around. "Just a minute." Standing up, he walked over to take samples from the milk brought in by two farmers.

"Something's wrong with Mr. Bloomquist," said Kate.

When the short, stocky man returned to them, he filled the tub with butter. Folding the liner across the top, he set the wooden cover in place.

What's the matter? Kate wondered. *He acts as if we aren't here.*

Anders tried to speak, but Mr. Bloomquist looked around, as though saying, "Wait till the farmers are gone."

Taking four tin strips, he nailed the cover in place, then stamped it with the name and address of the creamery. Below that he wrote a shipping number.

By the time the two farmers left, Anders was tapping his foot, clearly tired of waiting. Mr. Bloomquist nailed the last tub shut, then led them into the smaller room. Dropping into his chair, he said, "Now, let's hear what's going on."

Erik and Anders pulled up benches, and Kate told the buttermaker about the nighttime visitor.

Mr. Bloomquist shook his head. "Did Andrew leave the work sheets there?"

"I think so," answered Kate. "We didn't open the package, but Josie's father said Mr. Anderson brought papers."

The buttermaker moved restlessly in his chair. "It's one thing for someone to steal the cream checks. They're small, and the thief might get by, cashing them in different places. But why would he take the ledger? And why would he want the work sheets?"

As though too nervous to sit still, Mr. Bloomquist jumped up and paced the floor. Finally he came to a stop in front of Kate. "As long as he's searched Swensons' house, maybe that's the safest place to leave the papers. At least till Andrew gets back. But how did the man know where to look?"

Kate bit her lip. Should she say something about Leroy Fenton and Gunnar Grimm standing behind the butter churn? Was one of them guilty, or both? Or neither one? Kate couldn't prove a thing, and she might blame an innocent man.

Once more Mr. Bloomquist started pacing. Though a young man, his face looked old with worry. "When I got this job in November, I never dreamed it'd be like this. But there's more."

Striding to the doorway, Mr. Bloomquist looked around the large room, then shut the door. As he sat down, Kate, Anders, and Erik drew close.

Even so, Mr. Bloomquist spoke so low that Kate could barely hear. "Of all the things that have happened, this is the worst!"

14

The Butter Tub Disaster

*T*he buttermaker ran his fingers through his hair. "What a time for Andrew to be gone. I've never needed him more!"

"What's wrong?" Kate found it hard to believe anything could be worse than what had already happened.

"When we finish packing the butter tubs, we set them in the cold room," Mr. Bloomquist explained. "This morning I didn't feel right about the butter packed yesterday. I did something I've never done before. I opened a tub. The butter looked all right, but I tasted it." His voice rose in anger. "It was salty. Too salty to eat!"

Kate looked at Erik, and Erik looked at Anders. No one spoke.

Again Mr. Bloomquist ran his fingers through his hair. "What if I'd sent out those tubs of butter? Who would buy from us again?"

"Has anyone got something against you?" asked Erik. "Like a grudge, I mean?"

Mr. Bloomquist shrugged. "I don't know. I've wondered if

someone's trying to ruin me. But I don't have any enemies. I've been here only since November. Whoever spoiled the butter did it in just a few minutes."

"What do you mean?" Kate asked.

"When I finish churning a batch of butter, I check it for quality. Yesterday I tasted the butter, and it was exactly right. Then Gunnar Grimm called me into this room. When I returned, I filled the tubs."

"You were away from the butter for just a few minutes?" Erik asked.

"Not very long. I took a sample from a farmer too. In that time someone came in, threw in a large amount of salt, and churned it enough to mix it."

"The tubs you just packed—they're good butter?" Erik asked.

"They're good, all right. That's why I closed them up. But every tub packed yesterday had too much salt."

Just then Kate remembered something. "When Mr. Anderson talked about a contest, what did he mean?"

"There's a state buttermaker's contest next week. The creamery board wants me to enter."

"Is there a prize?" Anders asked.

"The largest amount ever offered by the state buttermaker's convention." Picking up a newspaper, Mr. Bloomquist pointed to an article.

Anders whistled. "$1,139.40! That's a lot of money."

"It would be divided among the winners. If I were a winner, it would give our creamery a good name."

"Something you need right now," Erik said. He stood up. "Anders and I need to get back to work."

But Kate had another question. "Was this butter supposed to go to the contest?"

Mr. Bloomquist shook his head. "No, to New York. But if a batch was ruined once, it could happen again. We might not even know for a while."

Kate felt more uneasy all the time. How could she find out what she needed to know?

"Mr. Bloomquist," she said slowly, "Mr. Fenton works for you, doesn't he?"

"Part time, learning the business. He's a good worker, knows what he's doing. Yesterday he was gone, harvesting ice."

Except for a few minutes, thought Kate, remembering again how she'd seen Mr. Fenton near the churn. Soon after, Mr. Grimm must have called the buttermaker into this room. Were the two men working together? Or did someone else spoil the butter?

"What about Mr. Grouch?" Anders asked, as though sensing Kate's thoughts. "I mean, Gunnar Grimm. You trust him?"

The buttermaker drew back, as if offended by the question. "Certainly. He's new around here, but he's trustworthy."

As Anders and Erik headed for the door, the buttermaker called to them. "The man who usually hauls butter to Grantsburg has the flu. Want to take your team tomorrow, Erik? Good money in it for you."

"Sure thing," Erik said. "This is our last day harvesting ice. The men we filled in for are coming back."

When Kate reached home, Mama had cut out her new dress. Her nimble fingers moved swiftly as she pinned the pieces together. "The cloth is beautiful!" Mama told Kate as she opened her arms for a hug.

But Kate saw the worry in Mama's eyes. Lars was still coughing, and coughing hard. Again Kate read to him from *Call of the Wild*.

That evening, while doing chores, Kate told Anders what she'd seen the day before.

"Mr. Grouch?" asked her brother. "And LeRoy Fenton? Somehow those two men keep popping up. I wish I could keep a better eye on them."

———

On her way to the barn the next morning, Kate read the thermometer. Thirty-four degrees below zero, Fahrenheit. Long before sunup, she and Anders milked the cows. When Erik drove into the yard, he helped Anders load the milk cans into the sleigh.

Erik wore his father's long coonskin coat. A warm cap covered his brown hair. With his forehead, nose, and chin wrapped in a heavy scarf, only his eyes showed.

Just then Lutfisk bounded up. "Erik!" said Anders, pointing to his friend. But the dog faced Erik and barked.

"He doesn't recognize your clothes," Anders said.

Erik pulled off a leather glove and stretched out his hand. "Come here, Lutfisk. It's me—Erik."

Again the dog barked. Anders pointed. "Go to Erik."

Wagging his tail, but still cautious, Lutfisk walked over. Erik let him smell his hand.

"Good dog," said Anders. "Let's try it again."

When he felt satisfied with what Lutfisk was learning, Anders led the others into the kitchen. While Erik warmed up by the cookstove, Kate and Anders pulled on every warm piece of clothing they owned. Anders wore Papa's long fur coat, while Kate put on Anders's sheepskin jacket. It hung down, well past her knees, which was just what she wanted.

Mama watched as they pulled on wool mittens. "If that cold air touches your face more than a minute, your skin will freeze," she warned. "And you're going all the way to Grantsburg?"

"We don't want to worry you, Mama." For once Anders didn't tease. "The man who usually takes the butter is sick."

Mama shook her head. "Do everything you can to be careful."

"We will, Mama," Anders promised.

Kate wrapped a scarf around her face, leaving only slits for her eyes. Carrying bricks warmed in the oven, she went outside.

"*Great* day for a trip!" Erik exclaimed as he followed Kate. Through the scarf covering his mouth, his voice sounded muffled. With all his heavy clothing, he moved slowly, yet he managed to help Kate onto the seat at the front of the sleigh.

Erik set the packed lunch in the back. Mama made sure they wouldn't go hungry. Though wrapped in blankets, the food would be frozen long before they reached Grantsburg.

"It'll get warmer this afternoon," Anders called to Mama, as he left the house. "Might even get up to ten below!"

The boys sat down on either side of Kate, and Erik flicked the reins. Queen and Prince headed out with the bells on their harness jingling.

During their drive to Trade Lake, the eastern sky turned red, then orange and gold. When they reached the creamery, Kate climbed down to warm up.

Mr. Bloomquist opened a door. LeRoy Fenton and Gunnar Grimm were with him. As the three men rolled out the sixty-pound tubs of butter, Erik and Anders loaded them onto the sleigh. Then all of them came in to warm up at the steam boiler.

"God dag, god dag!" said Anders, as he pulled off his mittens.

Kate glanced sideways at him. Her brother sounded as if he were saying "good dog." But he seldom spoke the Swedish greeting. What was his reason now?

"A good day to go to Grantsburg," Anders continued.

A slow smile eased onto Mr. Fenton's face. He pulled off the cap that covered his sandy-colored hair.

Erik looked even more alert than usual. Kate wondered if he and Anders had planned something?

"You know what I like about this cold?" Anders asked. "I like watching the steam rise from the horses' nostrils. Dragon breath, I call it!"

Kate saw a corner of Mr. Grimm's mouth turn up. She felt surprised. According to Anders, the man always looked as grim as his name.

"But you know what's best of all?" Anders went on. "When it's this cold, I like going to school just to see who didn't make it."

The hint of a smile appeared in Mr. Grimm's eyes. Even as it came, the look disappeared.

Did I imagine it? wondered Kate. *No. I don't think so.*

Anders summed it up. "Yup, a good day to go to Grantsburg, all right!"

"When it's thirty-four below, I just want to go home," Erik said.

"Home? Where's home to you, Mr. Fenton?" Anders asked.

Ah ha! thought Kate. *So that's what this is all about.*

"Home? Why, out east," answered Mr. Fenton smoothly. He stroked his mustache.

"Out east? Where about?" asked Anders quickly, the drawl gone from his voice. "What town?"

Mr. Fenton hesitated. "Philadelphia," he said. "You know, the city of brotherly love."

"Right, right." Anders turned to Mr. Grimm. "And you, Mr. Grouch? I mean—" Anders flushed red to the roots of his blond hair.

"Yes?" Mr. Grimm sounded dangerously calm. Yet the hint of a smile returned to his eyes. "Are you speaking to me?"

Clearing his throat, Anders started again. "Yes, sir, I'm speaking to you, sir. Do you have a family?"

Now he's polite, thought Kate.

"I'm staying with Reverend Pickle," answered Mr. Grimm with his gravelly voice.

"You're new, too?" Kate blurted out. "How come everyone harvesting ice is new at it?"

But no one gave her an answer. Pulling on their heavy coats, Mr. Grimm and Mr. Fenton started out of the room.

"Have to admit I'm relieved to see this butter go," Mr. Bloomquist said to Anders and Erik. "Be sure the tubs don't get banged up. I want them to look good when they reach New York. And get a receipt at the train."

Minutes later, Erik turned his horses toward Grantsburg. Queen and Prince stepped out, pulling the loaded sleigh as though it were no work at all.

Soon the horses left the road and started across a field. During the winter, farmers left their gates open. People cut through fields and woods to take the shortest way to town.

A rein in each hand, Erik talked to Queen and Prince, and their ears turned to the sound of his voice. Seeing how he guided the horses, Kate thought about why she liked Erik. Always he seemed to watch out for her. On her birthday, he had surprised her.

"You're different, Kate," he had said.

"Different?" Kate wasn't sure what he meant. "Awful?" She felt afraid to ask.

"Different from other girls. Better," Erik explained. "Very special."

In the frigid air the memory of his words warmed Kate. It didn't matter that he looked strange bundled against the cold.

Inside the layers of clothing, the warm cap, and the wool scarf was a special friend.

In the early morning sunlight the crust on the snow shimmered like ice. Through the scarf covering her mouth, Kate breathed deep. The problems at home and the creamery dropped away. Almost it seemed as if Kate had imagined them. Almost, but not quite.

Whenever they drove into a woods, she felt warmer, sheltered from the wind. Yet by now the bricks at her feet felt cold. Her toes tingled, then grew numb. Erik stopped the horses and told Kate to get down.

"Get down?" she asked.

"Walk, or you'll freeze. You have to walk to get warm."

Knotting the reins around a post at the front of the sleigh, Erik dropped to the ground. So did Anders.

"Giddyup!" Erik called to Queen and Prince. Avoiding the deep snow on either side, he and Anders and Kate walked in the packed down snow behind the sleigh.

If they came to a hill, Erik climbed onto the sleigh. Taking the reins, he made sure the horses didn't move too fast. Now and then he let Kate ride. Before long, all of them walked once more. Yet by the time they reached Grantsburg, Kate felt the coldest she'd ever been.

At the train depot, a refrigerated car waited on a side track.

"No need for ice today," Erik said, as he pulled alongside. Climbing down, he and Anders started transferring the tubs of butter into the railroad car.

Kate carried their lunch into the station. Inside the women's waiting room she set the food basket next to the potbellied stove to let the sandwiches thaw. Pulling off her mittens, she warmed her hands, standing as close to the wood stove as she dared.

Nearby, a woman sat on one of the wooden benches, comforting a crying baby. Another young child clung to his mother as they waited for the train.

Through the large window, Kate watched Anders and Erik shoulder the heavy tubs of butter. The sleigh was almost empty when Erik returned to the railroad car. Picking up a tub he'd set down, he shook it.

Shake a sixty-pound tub? thought Kate. *Why?* She couldn't even lift something that heavy.

As Erik put the tub aside, Anders finished unloading the sleigh. The station agent joined them to count the tubs of butter. Thirteen, fourteen, fifteen.

A moment later Erik picked up the mysterious tub and followed the agent into the depot. As Kate joined the boys in the office, the man made out a receipt.

"Do you have a hammer I can borrow?" Erik asked.

When the agent gave him one, Erik picked up the tub. "C'mon," he said, and Kate and Anders followed him outside.

"Where you going?" asked Kate. The boys couldn't enter the women's waiting room, and she wasn't allowed in the waiting room set aside for men and boys.

On the long platform, Anders pushed open a large sliding door. Erik and Kate followed him into another part of the station, the freight room. As Erik set down the heavy tub, Kate looked around.

In the light from the partly opened door, she saw wooden barrels and boxes of freight. At the moment there was no one there to watch what they were doing.

One by one, Erik pried up the metal strips on the butter tub. As Anders lifted the cover, Kate peered inside.

"Rocks!" she exclaimed. "Why would someone fill a tub with rocks?"

"Shhh!" said Erik, as though wanting to take no chances of anyone hearing them. He lifted out some of the rocks.

Lodged at the bottom of the tub, a gray book stood on end. A gray book with green corners. Was it the stolen ledger?

15

Sunday Deadline

*A*nders whistled softly. "It must be the creamery ledger!"

A grin lit Erik's face as he winked at Kate. Carefully he removed enough rocks to pull out the large book. When he turned the pages, Kate saw neatly written names and amounts.

"We really found it!" Kate exclaimed, keeping her voice low.

Before long they shivered with cold in the unheated freight room. Erik replaced the book and the rocks. Putting on the cover, he nailed down the metal strips and stood up.

"Be right back," he said quietly, lifting the tub to his shoulder. But his eyes looked excited.

Acting as if nothing important were happening, Erik strolled across the platform and over to his sleigh. Setting the tub inside, he covered it with a heavy horse blanket. Then he led Queen and Prince to the livery barn across the tracks.

When Erik returned to the freight room, he joined Kate and Anders just inside the large sliding door.

Anders spoke in a voice too quiet for anyone on the platform to overhear. "We have to find Big Gust." He pushed back his thatch of blond hair.

"Let's wait a few minutes," Erik answered, just above a whisper. "I don't want to take any chances."

Together they watched as other men brought horses and sleighs alongside the refrigerated car.

"They bring butter from a long way around," Erik explained to Kate. "They come from Webster. Falun. Doctor's Lake. West Sweden Creamery used to come here. Now they ship out on Frederic's new Soo Line."

A few minutes later, Anders nudged Kate. "See that man with a small mustache? That's Oscar Thorssen. Kind of a celebrity around here. Took the first prize at the Northern Wisconsin State Fair in 1898."

"For making butter?"

"Yup. When Mr. Thorssen won, he was only twenty-four years old."

"He's got the most butter of all," Erik said. "Twenty-eight tubs."

From the distance Kate heard a train whistle. The Blueberry Special! The whistle sounded again, closer this time and piercing the below-zero air.

Soon the engine puffed around the bend near the Hickerson Mill. Billows of black smoke rose from the large stack. Brakes hissed, releasing steam. Iron squealed on iron, and the engine came to a stop.

Working quickly in the frigid air, trainmen separated the engine from the freight and passenger cars. The engine moved farther on, then backed onto another track.

Stamping her feet in the cold, Kate leaned out of the sliding door to watch. The engine moved onto a section of track above a shallow pit. Using long levers and walking in a half circle, two men turned the track until the engine faced the direction from which it came.

Kate laughed, remembering the first time she'd seen the turntable. "Like Mama says, that Blueberry Special is really special!"

But Anders wasn't listening. He seemed miles away, gazing at the refrigerated car. Finally the men slammed the door shut and coupled that car to the rest of the train. Only then did Anders look away.

"I don't see Big Gust around," he said.

A seven-foot, six-inch-tall Swede, Gust Anderson was the Grantsburg village marshall. Because of his great height, the marshall lived in the fire hall. On more than one occasion he'd helped Kate and Anders.

"I'll keep an eye on the train till it leaves," Erik said.

By the time the Blueberry Special blew its departing whistle, Anders returned, saying, "He's not at the fire hall."

When he asked the station master where to find Big Gust, the man pointed away from the station. "He takes most of his meals at Walfrid Johnson's."

When Kate, Anders, and Erik went outside again, the air seemed warmer. As they set off for the building a short distance away, snow started to fall.

The minute they found themselves alone on the street, Anders exclaimed, "What a funny hiding place for a ledger!"

Erik grinned from ear to ear. "The thief would have sent it to New York!"

"How did you know that tub was different?" asked Kate.

"It weighed just the same," Erik said. "But when I put the tub down, I heard a sound. A rock rolling, I suppose. It was so cold we were moving really fast. I could have missed it."

"Three men helped you load the butter," Kate said. "Mr. Bloomquist. Mr. Fenton. Mr. Grimm. Which one put the ledger in the tub?"

"Not Mr. Bloomquist," said Erik. "He'd hurt himself by doing something like that."

Kate agreed. She'd come to like the buttermaker. "Yesterday he wasn't acting. He was upset."

"So that leaves two of 'em—Grouchy Grimm and LeRoy Fenton," Anders said. "I bet it's Mr. Grimm. Did you see how he sidestepped my questions? That's what he did every time we worked together. What's he got to hide?"

But Kate shook her head. "I think it's LeRoy Fenton." She looked up at Erik. "What do you think?"

As they came to a large frame building, Erik grinned. "I think it could be either one."

Walfrid Johnson had his blacksmith shop on the ground floor.

His family lived on the floor above. Anders led Kate and Erik up the stairs on the outside wall.

A short woman with a warm smile opened the door. "Come in, come in. Get out of the cold."

Several people sat around a large square table in the dining room. Big Gust was one of them. A woman stood next to him, serving food. Though he was sitting down, Gust was as tall as the woman standing beside him.

Seeing Kate and the boys, he called out, *"God dag!"*

When Kate walked closer, he looked down at her. "Little girl? What can I do for you?"

"I'm not a little girl!" Kate told him, flipping her long braid over her shoulder. "Not even if I'm short for my age!"

Big Gust's rumbling laugh came from deep in his chest. "You're right, young woman. Just like I'm not a big man! But what can I do for you and these tall boys with you?" He winked at Anders and Erik.

"We need to talk," Anders said.

The marshall's grin disappeared. "One minute," he said. Pouring his coffee into his saucer, he let it cool. As soon as he finished his meal, he unfolded his long frame and stood up.

Even now, after seeing Big Gust half a dozen times, Kate felt surprised by his height. The size of his large hands and feet fit with his tall frame.

Big Gust shrugged into his blue coat and started down the outside stairs. "It's too cold to talk here," he said. He led them to the fire hall.

There Gust made himself comfortable in an oversized chair. "What's wrong?" he asked with his deep laugh. "Somehow you attract trouble like bees to honey."

As Kate and the boys found chairs, Big Gust leaned forward to listen.

"Not good, not good," he said at last. "The one you really need to see is the sheriff, Charlie Saunders. But he's gone for the day. And you say Andrew Anderson number 3 talked to him?"

Anders nodded. "But Mr. Anderson is in North Branch. He doesn't know what just happened."

Big Gust rubbed his large chin. "Worst of all, this time of year we could have some mighty stormy weather. If we get a bad wind, you won't be able to get to town for help."

The marshall's blue eyes looked thoughtful. "Tell you what to do. If you can't get the sheriff, go to Reverend Pickle."

"The marrying man of Trade Lake?" Erik asked.

Big Gust nodded. "One and the same. Seldom a week goes by that he doesn't have a wedding or funeral. He's getting up in years now, but when he was a young man he was a detective."

"*Reverend Pickle?*" asked Anders.

"Yah, certainly," said the marshall. "Reverend Pickle. If you need help, he'll know what to do."

Before they left, Big Gust reached into his large pockets for peanuts in the shell. "Hold out your hands," he said and filled Kate's hands, then those of Anders and Erik.

As they went out the door, Big Gust offered a warning. "Whoever the thief is, be careful. He sounds like a bad one."

When Anders, Kate, and Erik returned to the train station, they ate their lunch, then climbed back on the sleigh. As Queen and Prince headed out of Grantsburg, new snow swirled around them.

"I've been thinking," Kate said.

"*Thinking?*" asked Anders.

Kate paid no attention. "I think Mr. Grimm is a different person from what he seems to be."

Anders looked ready to poke fun at anything she said, but Erik seemed to listen.

"Good? Bad? How do you mean, *different*?" he asked.

"I don't know." Kate was still wondering about it. "I just believe he's not what he seems."

Anders laughed, but Kate kept on. "Whoever the thief is, why would he send the ledger to New York?"

"Come to think of it, what else could he do?" Erik asked. "With the ground frozen, he can't bury it. It's too big to hide in a milk can."

"What if he had thrown it in a hole in the ice?" asked Kate. "Would it wash up on shore in spring?"

"Whoever the thief is, he's mighty smart," Erik said slowly. "He's got everything figured out."

"There's something else that bothers me," Kate answered. "Don't you think the thief has given us some kind of signal? He sent the ledger to New York, where it's sure to be seen. Doesn't that mean he's ready to leave Trade Lake?"

The grin disappeared from Anders's face. "Gotcha!" he exclaimed. "The ledger would have reached New York by Monday morning. At least that's when they put the tubs on the market."

"And if someone opened that tub—" Kate pulled up her scarf to protect her face against the cold. "Big trouble!"

As they passed through a clean-cut field, gusts of snow whirled around them, filling in the packed-down trail. As Queen and Prince headed into the drifts, snow sprayed up against their forelegs. Steam rose from their nostrils.

Erik let the horses set their own pace. "A ledger in a butter tub is real strange. Whoever found it probably wouldn't waste the time it takes for letters to go back and forth. He might even send a telegram to the Grantsburg train depot."

"The thief knows that," said Kate. "He's been smart about everything else."

"Except for using rocks in a butter tub." Erik grinned. "Now if it were me, I'd have put in some sawdust to deaden the sound."

But Anders no longer joked. "If we've got it figured right, the thief will leave town by Sunday night."

"That means we have only four days to find him," said Kate. "Or we might never find out who he is!"

16

Thin Ice!

*T*hat also means we have only four days to find the milk can," said Erik.

Anders scowled. "Or the thief will take the checks with him when he leaves. If he goes to a city where he's not known, he might be able to cash them."

A rein in each hand, Erik turned the horses onto a trail through the woods. The sheltering trees offered welcome relief from the wind. Even so, Kate's fingers tingled with cold, then grew numb. Before long, all of them climbed down to walk behind the sleigh.

"So what do we do with the ledger?" Kate asked.

"Well, we can't take it to the creamery." Anders felt certain about that. "The thief would just steal it again. Let's wait till Andrew Anderson comes back. We'll ask him."

Together they agreed that Anders would hide the butter tub in the Windy Hill barn.

"There's something we still don't know," said Erik. "Why does someone want to get even with Mr. Bloomquist?"

Some time later they climbed onto the sleigh. Kate huddled under a heavy horse blanket in the back. Her thoughts were as miserable as her cold body. Every grown-up who knew about the robbery had warned them, and with good reason.

When at last they came to the Nordstrom mailbox, Anders called out, "Letter for you, Kate!"

Like a turtle coming from its shell, Kate poked out her head. A letter just for her? Papa's handwriting! He must have written the day he received her letter. In spite of the biting wind, Kate felt warm.

"I'll be over tomorrow," Erik said as he pulled up outside the Nordstrom barn. "We'll look for the milk can again."

"And we'll find it!" Anders exclaimed. Swinging down the butter tub, he started for the barn, then turned back to Erik. "Let Lutfisk follow you home. In the morning, early, I'll try sending him over with a message."

When Kate entered the kitchen, she could no longer feel her feet. Pulling off her boots, she curled up close to the cookstove. As her toes returned to life, they prickled, as though touched by a thousand needles.

With her fingers still awkward from the cold, Kate opened her letter. Papa had written in English, using a bold, strong script.

As Mama, Anders, and Tina clustered around, Kate remembered Lars. "Let's read it where he can hear," she said.

In the bedroom Kate began to read.

Dear Kate,

Thank you for your letter. It was good for a father to hear from his daughter. I miss you very much.

Remember how we talked at Christmas about the big loads of logs the sleighs carry? This week I saw a sleigh carrying 56 giant logs. That's 37,120 board feet of lumber!

You might wonder how only four horses can pull such a load. Last fall men built roads of ice into the woods. For weeks they hauled water to make the road one-foot thick. Then other men cut ruts in the ice. The sleigh runners slide in those ruts. On hills the men lay down straw to slow the sleigh so it doesn't run over the horses.

Kate looked up. "That's why Erik had that accident! There

should have been straw on that road! Maybe the load of ice wouldn't have shifted."

She returned to reading:

> *When I came back after Christmas, I got a new job. Now I'm what is called a water-tank conductor. I work at night and repair the road of ice. In our camp we have two tank sleighs, and I use the smaller one.*
>
> *Our horses, Dolly and Florie, help me pull barrels of water up a skid to fill the tank on the sleigh. Then I drive up and down the road. Wherever the ice is thin or dirt shows through, I lift long poles to unplug the holes in the tank. Water runs out and fills the bad spots. That water freezes to make the road good again.*
>
> *To see in the dark I light lard oil torches on the corners of the water tank.*

Then Kate came to a blank space. Had the paper been wet, then wiped dry? Glancing ahead, she stopped reading aloud. "This is just for me," she said finally.

Folding the letter, Kate took it to her room where she could be alone. Wrapping herself in a quilt, she huddled on the grate that let in heat from the stove below. Then she reread the last page of the letter.

> *When my first wife Anna died, I was very sad. I didn't know God had something good in store for me. You prayed for a father and didn't know it would be me. When I married your mama, you became my new, special daughter.*
>
> *I can never take the place of your Daddy O'Connell. I want you to remember him and what a fine man he was. At the same time, I feel honored to be your second father.*
>
> *When you are afraid, remember that you also have a Heavenly Father. He has promised you something: "Fear thou not; for I am with thee: be not dismayed, for I am thy God: I will strengthen thee; yea, I will help thee" Isaiah 41:10.*
>
> *Even when I cannot be with you, your Heavenly Father is.*
>
> *With love to my special daughter,*
PAPA

Kate stared at Papa's words. *When you are afraid? How did*

he know? She had tried to make him feel good, instead of telling how scared she really felt.

For a long time she held the letter, thinking about the verse. *Fear thou not; for I am with thee.* Each time Kate repeated the words, she felt better inside, even warm.

Though she hadn't told Papa how she felt, he somehow knew. Kate felt cared for by God himself.

————

When Kate read Papa's letter again the next morning, she found a small slip of paper that had slipped down inside the envelope. It read:

P.S. I'll start home January 31.

Running downstairs, Kate told Mama, "Papa's coming the 31st! That's today!"

Her mother's quiet smile lit her eyes. "And it's sooner than I expected. Many of the men will work longer."

By noon the thermometer showed eighteen degrees above zero. After the temperature of the day before, the weather felt warm and balmy.

When Erik skied over after lunch, he held out a piece of paper. "Lutfisk did it! I got the message from you!"

Seeming to know they talked about him, the dog jumped up, wanting attention.

Anders grinned with pride. "We'll send him over whenever we need you." Kneeling down, he scratched Lutfisk behind the ears. The dog woofed and licked his master's face.

Kate and the boys decided to search two small lakes they hadn't tried before. With Anders carrying a long pole, they skied across country. Whenever they found a hole in the ice, they felt new hope. Using the pole, Anders or Erik poked around in the water, looking for the milk can.

As they skied toward the second lake, snowflakes drifted lazily to the ground. Soon dark branches were outlined in white. By the time they finished searching, pine trees wore a new robe.

Anders sighed. "Well, we've done our best." He looked cold and discouraged. "That's the last of the lakes close by. Maybe we should start over again."

Erik shook his head. "Not today. The wind's coming up."

"Let's go to Little Trade Lake," Anders said.

Kate felt uneasy. "That's out of the way." It would take time to ski to Windy Hill Farm, and Erik's house was farther yet.

Putting on her skis, Kate started for home. Erik followed, but Anders wasn't ready to give up.

"We have to cross Rice Lake anyway," he said. "Let's look there again."

When they reached the southwestern corner, they followed the trail through the boggy area. As they cut slantwise across the lake, Erik took the lead. Soon he pointed off to the right. "Something's over there! See those markers?"

About fifty feet from shore, four small pine trees stood upright in the snow. A skim of new ice covered what had been a large hole.

Taking off her skis, Kate walked as close to the hole as was safe. New snow dotted the thin ice, making it difficult to see.

Using the long pole, Erik struck the ice and broke it. As Kate peered down into the lake, she thought she saw a glimmer. Was that something just beneath the surface?

"Isn't that a milk can?" she asked.

"Might be." Erik sounded afraid to hope. He and Anders took turns poking around in the water with the long pole. No matter how hard they tried, they couldn't make the pole reach far enough.

Finally Erik skirted the thin ice and headed toward shore. Kate and Anders followed him.

Near a tall oak Erik pulled off his mittens and grabbed a stout branch that extended toward the lake. He pulled himself up onto the limb and crawled out to see better.

For a few seconds he stared into the dark water. "There!" he exclaimed finally. "There's a glimmer of metal in the water. Could be a can!"

Standing on shore, Anders and Kate moved around, trying to see what Erik meant. Soon Anders pointed toward the center of the hole. "Yup! That's it! See that round circle? Look hard. Isn't that a rim?"

Erik edged still farther out on the branch. "It's the bottom of a milk can, all right. Upside down, same as before."

"We found it!" whooped Kate.

"You betcha!" Anders stepped forward for a better look.

"We really did it!" Kate said, moving onto the ice.

Anders stretched out an arm, holding her back. "We haven't done anything yet!"

"So how do we get the can out?" asked Kate.

"That's the problem." Again Anders looked into the cold water. "Before, we had solid ice to stand on. This time we don't."

"The can's lined up with the tree," Erik called down. "Almost exactly in the center of the hole. There's at least ten feet of thin ice on every side."

"How did the thief get it there?" asked Kate.

"Probably threw it." Anders sounded unhappy. "We aren't playing around with an amateur. He's got good aim to land it where he did."

Slowly Erik started edging back along the tree limb. Close to the trunk he stopped and pulled something from a small sharp branch. Tucking it inside his pocket, he dropped to the ground.

When he reached Kate and Anders, Erik held out his find—a small piece of cloth.

"Part red, part black!" exclaimed Kate.

Erik nodded. "See the jagged edges? Looks like it's been torn from a mackinaw."

"So the thief was up that tree before you!"

"I think so." Erik pushed back his cap. "Way I figure it, he threw in the can, then checked to be sure it landed right."

"So all we have to do is look for a red and black mackinaw," Kate said. "That sounds simple enough."

"Except for one thing," Anders told her.

"What's that?"

"An awful lot of men in Burnett County have red and black mackinaws!"

Kate sighed. She knew Anders was right. And the two men they suspected most—Gunnar Grimm and LeRoy Fenton—both had one.

Still the piece of cloth offered a slim clue. "Not every man will have a *torn* mackinaw," Kate said.

Turning back to the hole, she gazed at the round metal rim just beneath the surface of the water. "Isn't there any way we can get the can out?"

"Not with the ice the way it is," Anders told her. "One wrong step, and we'd drop right through."

"Let's go for help," Kate said. "Now before the snow gets worse."

Putting on their skis, Kate, Anders, and Erik set off again, this time for the village of Trade Lake. Erik took the lead, retracing their tracks.

As they crossed Rice Lake, Kate felt the change in the weather. Whirlwinds caught the new snow, spraying it through the air. Like small grains of sand, the snow pelted her face. If this kept up, they wouldn't be able to reach the creamery.

"Erik!" Kate shouted, fighting to speak. "Erik!" she called again.

But the wind took her words, flinging them away. She wasn't even sure if Erik heard.

17

Lars's Question

*B*ending her head against the wind, Kate struggled to keep up with Erik. Near the southwestern shore of the lake their earlier tracks were blurred. Erik kept on, avoiding the creek, and finding the path. As they entered the shelter of woods, the wind stilled.

Kate breathed deep. Yet even here snow had piled up. The woods were dark, the sky gray with falling snow.

When they came out from the trees, the white wind swooped across the open field. Driving snow stung Kate's cheeks. Her eyes watered, but she didn't want to give up. Wrapping her scarf around her face, she skied on.

A few minutes later Erik stopped them. "We can probably reach Trade Lake. But if we go that far, we won't get home. Everyone will wonder what happened to us."

"Mama knows we're smart enough to get out of a storm," Anders said.

"Mama will worry about us," replied Kate. "And Erik's mother will worry about him." Like Papa Nordstrom, Erik's father was away, working at a logging camp.

"If we don't get help now, the hole in the ice will freeze over," Anders said. "The thief can come back, take the can, and leave town."

Anders was right, Kate knew. Yet as she opened her mouth to agree, another gust of wind struck her. She staggered, then caught her breath.

"I'll go for help," Anders said to Kate. "You and Erik ski home. Tell Mama I'm safe."

"No!" Erik objected. "The storm is getting worse all the time. If you lose your way, you could miss the town."

"And what if your bad ankle gives out?" asked Kate. "There'll be no one to help you."

Anders sighed, clearly unwilling to stop.

"Let's stick together," Kate said. "That means going home."

She and Erik turned, starting toward Windy Hill Farm. After a short distance, Kate looked back. Anders stood there, as though trying to make up his mind. In the snow that swirled between them, he started to disappear.

"C'mon, Anders," Kate called into the wind.

But Anders heard. Pushing off, he followed Kate.

On the far side of the woods they once again skied onto Rice Lake. Drawing close to the hole where they'd found the milk can, Erik stopped.

By the time the storm ended, drifts might cover the small pine trees. The hole in the ice would be frozen, and the milk can hidden. Would they be able to find it again?

For a moment they stood there, facing the tall oak. Through the driving snow, Kate stared toward shore.

"One branch reaches out over the water," she said finally. But was that enough? Other trees dotted the shoreline. Would they mistake one of them for the tall oak?

"Pine trees," she said, pointing. "One left of the oak. Several on the right." She tried to remember the distance, to mark the spot in her mind.

Erik nodded, then Anders. Taking the most direct route, they struck out for home. As the wind clutched their clothing, they bent almost double, skiing on.

Soon the early winter darkness blended with the falling snow. Kate lost sight of Erik. Following the tracks of his skis, she caught up. Even Anders hurried now, the cap he usually wore at a jaunty angle pulled low over his forehead.

As they started up the bank along the shore, Anders stumbled. *His ankle,* Kate thought. *What if he hurts it again?* But Anders caught himself. He followed close behind, as though making sure Kate didn't lose her way.

At the top of the hill, the farmhouse faded into the swirling snow. Then Kate saw a glow of light. Mama had placed three candles in the window. Their warmth reached out, across the wind and cold.

Three, thought Kate. *One for Anders. One for me. Is the third candle for Erik?*

Then Kate remembered. January 31. Today Papa started home. Was he out somewhere in this awful storm?

————

During supper Kate felt bone-tired from skiing, but Mama looked even more weary. All afternoon she had sewed on the new blue dress. With Lars sick, she often missed sleep.

"I'll read to him," Kate told Mama after washing the dishes.

Once again she opened the pages of *Call of the Wild.* Each day she and Lars had followed the adventures of the strong dog, Buck. By now they were almost to the end of the book.

When Kate finished the last chapter, Lars lay with eyes closed, as if too tired to hold them open. Yet Kate knew he wasn't sleeping.

At last he spoke. "Kate?"

His voice was so soft that she leaned forward. "I'm here."

"Kate, did you like reading about Buck?"

"I liked Buck," Kate said carefully, not wanting to spoil the story for him. "He was a special dog—a smart dog, wasn't he?"

Lars nodded. "A *magnificent* dog."

Kate smiled. Lars seemed so small, lying there in bed, that the word seemed bigger than he was.

For a moment Lars was quiet. "That's what he was—a magnificent dog. Even when people were mean to him."

"Did he remind you of Lutfisk?" Kate asked.

"In some ways," said Lars, his eyes still closed. "But I'm glad our dog is different."

After a time Lars spoke again. "'Course we've always been

nice to Lutfisk. We've taken good care of him." His voice sounded drowsy.

Kate sat down on a chair next to the bed, waiting for Lars to fall asleep. Instead he opened his eyes. "I don't like the way the story ends. John Thornton was nice to Buck. He treated him right. I don't like that John Thornton died."

"I'm glad you felt that way," said Kate. "I did too."

"You did?" Lars's blue eyes seemed too bright. "You know what, Kate? When I grow up, I'm going to be a writer."

Kate smiled. "Just like I want to be an organist?"

"Yup. And I'm going to make stories end different."

The last word ended on a cough. As Lars tried to sit up, Kate pushed another pillow behind him. His body shook with coughing.

When he dropped back, Lars looked exhausted, his face flushed. Yet beneath his freckles, he also seemed strangely white.

What would we do without him? Kate wondered. The idea frightened her so much she could scarcely breathe.

"Kate?" Lars said softly. "How come you're different from the way you used to be?"

"Different?" asked Kate. "What do you mean?"

"You're not the same as when you first came here." Again Lars coughed. Pushing himself up, he leaned forward. In between the coughing, his breathing rattled. "My chest hurts," he said when able to speak.

Kate stood up and rubbed his back. Through his nightshirt Kate felt Lars's spine and ribs and his thinness. Then, thinking about his cough, she felt afraid.

When Lars lay back again he kept his eyes open. "You still get into all kinds of trouble," he said.

For a moment a grin lit his face. "Can't figure out how *anyone* can find so many mysteries to solve. But it's like—" He stopped, as though to think about it. "It's like God means something to you."

Then Kate knew what Lars was talking about. She remembered the day last fall when Tina could have been badly hurt because of something Kate did. On that day her whole life had changed.

Now Lars stared at her, his eyes unblinking. "Kate, do you love Jesus?" he asked.

Kate looked him straight in the eyes. "Yes, Lars, I love Jesus." It felt good to tell him, but she wondered, *Why does he want to know?*

In that moment her younger brother seemed very special to her. She reached out and took his hand. "Are you afraid, Lars?"

Lars nodded. A tear slid down his cheek. "I'm scared, Kate." His voice was so soft that she could barely hear. "I'm scared I'm going to die. Would I go to heaven? Am I good enough?"

Kate had never seen her brother so serious. Again she remembered the day she cried out, "Mama, I'm so awful!" Her mother had agreed, saying, "Yah, we are all awful." But then Mama explained that no one is perfect.

"Lars," Kate said, and her voice wavered. "You know how much God loves you. How He sent His Son Jesus to earth as a little baby."

Lars nodded. "And Jesus died for us on the cross."

"When we do wrong things, we can say we're sorry." Kate's voice was stronger now. "If we ask forgiveness, God *does* forgive us."

"Even you, Kate." Lars grinned weakly.

Kate grinned too, but she went on. "And Jesus takes away our sin. He forgets all about it."

For a time Lars was silent, seeming to think. "I believe that," he said finally, his voice little more than a whisper. "So will I go to heaven?"

Quick tears blurred Kate's vision. She could barely speak. "You'll go to heaven, Lars. Jesus will be with you, no matter what happens to you."

Lars closed his eyes. His face looked peaceful, and for a time he did not cough. Yet he held tight to Kate's hand.

18

The Lost Fiddle

For a long time Kate sat next to Lars's bed. When at last he fell asleep, his grip on her hand loosened. Kate fled to her room and cried.

The next morning she was first to enter the kitchen. Crossing the floor, she slipped and fell. When she lit a kerosene lamp, she found the reason.

"Ice?" she muttered. "On the kitchen floor?" Three feet from the cookstove, someone had spilled water. During the night it had frozen.

Quickly Kate started a fire in the stove. Then she discovered a long ridge of snow near the outside door. Taking a broom, she swept it up as though it were sand. Putting down a small rug, she blocked out the narrow crack beneath the door.

More snow lay on the window ledges, sifted in through cracks too small to see. As Kate cleaned up, her mother entered the kitchen.

Mama's face looked set and white. In spite of her growing weight, she moved quickly between the stove and table. But then she burned the oatmeal. Kate knew Mama's thoughts were far away.

As Anders and Kate walked to the barn for chores, the wind

swooped across the hill, striking them full force. Anders reached back and took Kate's hand, as though afraid she'd lose the way. Bent almost double against the wind, they crossed to the barn.

Anders held the door for Kate. When he let go, it crashed shut. For a moment they stood just inside, catching their breath.

Here, away from Mama, Kate could ask what she wanted to know. "Where do you think Papa is?"

Anders shook his head.

So he's worried too.

Kate tried again. "If Papa left camp before the blizzard started, how far would he get?"

"Depends on how deep the snow is and how big the drifts are."

"Are there towns along the way?"

"Not many."

"Houses?" Kate asked, her voice small.

"Some. They're far apart. But Papa's wise," Anders added quickly, as though trying to make her feel better. "He's like most farmers, smart about weather. He probably saw this coming."

"And went inside?"

Anders shrugged his shoulders. Lifting the cover of a bin, he took out oats for Wildfire. The mare's black coat was thick with winter hair. She nuzzled his jacket, but for the first time Kate could remember, Anders didn't talk to his horse.

All day long the wind blew. Kate wandered from room to room, thinking about Papa trying to get home. About the milk can in the lake. And about Lars. What if he needed a doctor?

During the afternoon Mama showed Kate how to cut the flannel cloth. Much as Kate wanted to make a few clothes for the baby, she couldn't keep her mind on it.

Anders looked just as restless as Kate felt. He, too, wandered between windows. Snow, driven against the glass, blocked the view.

In the strange half light Kate sat down at her organ. As she played familiar hymns, Tina came and stood beside her. In her small clear voice, she began to sing.

When Kate looked up, Mama sat nearby, the almost-finished dress forgotten in her lap. Staring at the snow-darkened windows, she bit her lip, then lifted her chin.

A gust of wind rattled the windows. In the nearby bedroom, Lars coughed from deep in his chest.

"It must be pneumonia," whispered Mama.

What'll we do? thought Kate. *What if we have to go for the doctor?*

Mama hurried to the bedroom. "Play some more, will you, Kate?"

When Kate finished the hymns she knew, she practiced the music Mr. Peters gave her. Thinking about the string band seemed the only bright spot in the day.

Late that afternoon Kate and Anders hurried through snow and early darkness to the barn. While Anders started milking, Kate fed the sheep and cows. Even here the wind howled around the corners.

Kate shivered. "I'm scared, Anders."

"About Lars? So am I."

His answer surprised Kate. Six feet tall and muscular from farm work, Anders seldom showed fear about anything.

"A lot of people die from pneumonia," said Kate.

"I know," answered Anders, his voice quiet. "Lars has never been strong. Not since the day he was born. From the time he was little, Mama taught me to watch out for him."

Again Kate felt surprised. Anders seldom mentioned his first mother.

"Lars always gets sick easier than the rest of us," Anders went on. "And he always takes longer to get well."

In the silence the wind shrieked through cracks in the barn. The ache in Kate's stomach tightened in a knot of fear.

"Anders?"

"Yup?"

"Does the wind ever stop?"

"Nope. Not till the storm's over."

"I don't like the wind." Kate shivered again. "I don't like looking out and seeing nothing but white."

"That's what Papa said."

"Papa?" asked Kate.

"At Christmas when he left for logging camp. That's what he said."

Kate remembered that day. From outside the farmhouse door, she had watched Papa leave. As he stood near the sleigh, he talked to Anders. Kate strained to hear, but the wind swallowed the words.

Now Anders turned from the cow he was milking. "Papa said, 'It's been a long time since Mama lived on a farm in winter. And Kate never has. They don't know what it's like when the wind blows all day and there's nothing to see but snow.' "

Kate stared at her brother. "Papa said that? He always knows, doesn't he? What else did he say?"

" 'Take care of 'em, Anders. Take care of Mama, and Tina, and Lars.' " Anders grinned. " 'And Kate.' "

"Take care of *me*? Papa knows I can take care of myself."

"Papa knows you need taking care of. Curious Kate—that's you. Always getting into something."

Kate tossed her head, and her long braid swung down her back. She wasn't sure if Anders was teasing or not. She was thirteen now and could take care of herself.

"Better put some wood in the tank heater, Kate."

"Why don't *you* do it?" she answered, tired of his orders. Besides, she hated going out in the dark.

"Sure thing," said Anders, standing up. "If you finish this cow."

Quickly Kate headed for the door. Though she'd learned to milk when Anders sprained his ankle, it still took her longer than she liked.

Outside, she hurried to the woodpile near the large tank for watering animals. A stove set inside the tank heated the water in winter.

The heater looked like a U with the sides pushed slightly down. At one end of the U, a stove pipe stretched above the water. At the other end, a stove lid covered the opening for loading wood. Lifting the lid, Kate dropped in small chunks of oak.

When she returned to the barn, Anders had moved on to

another cow. Taking a stool, Kate sat down to milk the cow next in line.

"Anders, what're you going to do about the string band?"

"Well, I'll join it." He sounded as though he wondered why Kate asked.

"You will?" Kate wished she could see her brother, but a cow stood between them. "What instrument will you play?"

"The fiddle, of course." His matter-of-fact voice made it seem there was no other choice.

"The *fiddle*?" Kate found it hard to believe she'd heard correctly. "That's a hard instrument to play. And you—"

She stopped, knowing she shouldn't go on.

"And me—I'm a country bumpkin. Is that what you're thinking?"

Kate felt a blush go to the roots of her hair. During her first week at Windy Hill Farm, she'd called Anders that name. Since then she'd learned he was anything but.

Yet a fiddle didn't fit with what she knew about him. *Anders? Playing a fiddle? With his big fingers and hands?*

"In fact," he continued, "if I can find it, there's a fiddle around here. Mama used to play."

"Your mother?" Kate asked, feeling more strange all the time. "Papa's first wife?"

Anders nodded.

"You never told me that."

"Lots of things I don't tell you," said Anders. "You don't know *everything* I know."

But Kate remembered last summer and the day of the big storm. It took all her courage to sing in front of Anders. "I thought you didn't like music."

"Well, you're wrong. Before she died, my mama started teaching me how to play. She said I had a good ear for it."

Kate wanted to laugh. But in the next moment she was glad she hadn't.

"I was starting to get good," said Anders. "Then Mama died. At first I played all the time. Then I couldn't stand to touch the fiddle. And I knew it bothered Papa to hear me. It reminded us both of Mama."

For a time Anders was silent. Kate heard only the sound of milk splashing into their pails. Then he stood up and walked around to Kate's side of the cow.

"One day I wrapped the fiddle in a cloth and gave it to Papa. I asked him to put it away for me. And he did."

"So you don't know where it is?" Kate stopped milking.

"All I know is that Papa would put it somewhere safe. Where it wouldn't be too hot or too cold. Where the wood wouldn't crack."

"How do you know?" Kate asked. Then she saw her brother's eyes. In the light of the kerosene lantern they seemed moist.

"When I gave it to Papa, he unwrapped the cloth. He felt the wood as though he wanted to touch something Mama loved. Then he wrapped the fiddle again and put it away."

Kate leaned closer to the quiet voice. "I think we should find that fiddle."

Anders answered slowly. "Kate, I'm scared. What if we find the fiddle, and I can't play it?"

Kate knew what he meant. He wasn't afraid that he couldn't play the notes. It was more than that. Could he play again, remembering his first mother and how it felt to lose her?

Then Kate felt sure of something. "You'll be able to play. It's what your mama would want you to do."

"You really think so?" Anders stared at Kate as though her answer were the most important thing in the world.

"I think so. Pretend you're playing for *her.*"

A strange expression crossed his face. Kate wasn't sure what it meant. Was this the Anders who never showed fear or tears?

Turning, he stalked away. With his back toward Kate, he stared out a window. For a long time he stood there, though Kate knew he couldn't see into the storm.

All her life she'd heard people say that men and boys shouldn't cry. Now she wondered, *Is that how Anders feels? That he can't cry, no matter what happens?*

When he returned to milking, Anders seemed his usual self. "I'll play the fiddle again," he said. "Yah sure, you betcha."

19

Another Warning

*T*hat night Kate and Anders searched for the lost fiddle. They had almost given up when Kate pulled a chair over to the cupboard in the pantry.

"I can't reach far enough," she called to Anders. "Come do it for me."

Sure enough, the fiddle lay on top of the cupboard, far back against the wall.

Climbing down from the chair, Anders opened the cloth and felt the wood. Without a word, he carried the fiddle into the front room, where he could be alone.

From the kitchen Kate listened, but heard no playing. When at last a note came, it sounded scratchy and out of tune.

Mama raised her eyebrows.

"It was his mother's," Kate explained. From that time on, Mama listened too.

As though Anders struggled to remember the fingering, there came a note, a pause, then another note. Sometimes he plucked the strings. Other times he drew his bow across. Then it sounded as if he was tuning the fiddle.

When Kate woke the next morning, she found herself buried deep beneath the quilts. As she pulled them away from her head, she saw her breath in the cold air.

After breakfast Anders went out to brush the snow off the windows. Yet the white wind still blew, pelting snow as though sand. Before long, the windows again gave only an eerie half light.

"It's Saturday," Kate told Anders when they were alone. "Papa started home Thursday—two days and two nights ago."

"And tomorrow's Sunday," answered her brother, as though unable to talk about Papa. On Sunday the thief would leave town.

That afternoon both Kate and Anders forgot everything except Lars. While Kate read to him, Lars started shaking with a chill. As he coughed, he held his chest.

"Oh, Kate, I hurt," he said when he could speak again. "It's such an awful pain."

Kate pushed another pillow under his back and put on more quilts, but Lars still trembled.

When she glanced up, Anders stood at the door, his eyes scared. Coming close to the bed, he flashed his lopsided grin. "You gotta get well, buddy."

Against the white pillowcase, Lars's hair seemed even redder than usual. His face looked pale, but he grinned for his brother.

Awkwardly Anders patted Lars on the shoulder. "When you're well again, we'll hitch Lutfisk to the sled. You can ride across the hills."

Lars's grin disappeared in a cough. Leaning forward, he coughed several more times. Kate handed him a handkerchief.

When it came away from Lars's mouth, Anders watched. As though unable to handle being there, he bolted from the room.

A short time later, Kate heard Anders tune the fiddle. Gradually the notes sounded clearer, then strong, even beautiful. Lars lay without speaking, but Kate saw his eyes and knew that he listened.

As Anders started a Swedish folk song, Mama came to the doorway. Halfway across the room, she stopped and tilted her head toward the music. The melody seemed to sing.

"It's good to remember," Mama whispered when Anders finished. "We're children of the Heavenly Father." Neither she nor Kate moved.

————

Early Sunday morning the family gathered near Lars's bed to have church together. When Mama asked Kate to read, she chose the words that Papa sent her: "Fear thou not, for I am with thee; be not dismayed; for I am thy God. . . ."

Glancing up, Kate saw Mama bite her lip. Kate read on: "I will strengthen thee; yea, I will help thee. . . ."

As they bowed their heads, Mama laid a gentle hand on Kate's arm. When they prayed for Lars, Mama moved her hand to his shoulder. "Jesus, in Thy name we ask Thee to heal Lars."

Then, as often before, Mama prayed for Papa. "Lord, we don't know where he is." Mama's voice broke, and she stopped.

Kate opened her eyes. Mama struggled for control.

"We don't know where he is, God," she went on. "But thou knowest. Thou art his Heavenly Father."

Her voice grew stronger. "We ask thee to take care of Papa. We ask thee to keep him warm and safe and bring him home to us soon. In thy name, Jesus, we pray. Ah-men."

When Mama stopped praying, no one spoke. Within the small circle around Lars's bed, it felt warm. Kate knew the warmth was love.

Then her brother's cough broke the silence. Again Kate heard the wind. It seemed to separate them from the rest of the world.

A short time later, Tina grew restless, and Kate led her to the kitchen. "Look!" Kate said to her little sister. "Jack Frost painted the windows last night."

Five-pointed stars filled one pane and snowflakes another. At a window covered with solid frost, Kate asked Tina, "Want to make footprints?"

Tina shrugged, not understanding Kate's English.

Balling her hand into a fist, Kate pressed the side of her little finger against the glass. The heat of her hand melted the frost. Using her thumb and fingers, she added a big toe and four smaller ones. Sure enough, there was a footprint!

Tina giggled, and started making her own prints in the frost.

"C'mon, Anders," called Kate. "We need some *big* feet."

Anders joined them, pressing his large hands against the glass. One after another, he placed footprints, until it seemed a person walked across the window.

Standing back to look, Tina giggled again.

An hour later, Kate lifted her head and listened. After three days of howling wind, the world seemed strangely still. The storm was over!

When Kate and Anders went outside to shovel, the clouds had disappeared. Drifts curled around the corners of the house. As far as they looked, they saw smooth, unbroken snow—snow that glistened in the sunlight.

"We are *buried*!" exclaimed Anders. Every trail and path had blown shut.

As they started toward the barn, Kate saw the relief in her brother's face. He even seemed to walk more quickly.

"You were scared, weren't you?" she asked.

Anders nodded, his blue eyes shading darker. "How do you get a doctor in a howling blizzard? How do you travel for miles when you can hardly get to the barn?"

"Maybe Papa will be able to get through."

"Maybe," said Anders. "I hope so."

They harnessed Wildfire, then hitched her to chains attached to a heavy log. As the mare moved ahead, the log dragged along the ground, smoothing out the snow and packing down the trail.

Soon after lunch, Kate heard the jingle of bells. Erik drove out of the woods and across the field between the two farms. He, too, dragged a log behind the Lundgren team of horses.

Waving at Kate, Erik turned Queen and Prince down the hill toward Rice Lake. Anders followed with Wildfire. When they returned, they had smoothed a trail all the way across Rice Lake.

"When we reached the road, we saw men working," said Anders. "Every few miles people will be out."

Mama looked hopeful. "Maybe Papa will come home."

And if we have to go for the doctor, we can, thought Kate.

When she and Anders were alone, Kate asked about the milk can. "Is it still there?"

"As far as we can tell. No footprints at least. But we can't get to Andrew Anderson's yet. Not till some time after dark when the men finish working on the roads."

Kate sighed. "We're out of time. It's Sunday night."

At dusk the first sleigh passed through the farmyard. The neighbor stopped at the house, asking, "Are you all right, Mrs. Nordstrom?"

Mama nodded her head, and said, "Yes, except for Lars."

Then came the question. "Have you heard from Carl?"

Mama's blue eyes clouded. Her *no* was even more quiet than her *yes*.

When Anders and Kate did the chores, she thought she heard another sleigh. Above the lowing of the cows, she listened, then decided she imagined it.

As they left the barn, the Milky Way lit a path through the sky. When Kate held out the lantern, she thought she saw something. Stopping, she set down her pail of milk.

Anders almost bumped into her. "What's the matter?"

Alongside the track, the wind had packed the snow into a drift. In the middle of the smooth whiteness, Kate saw letters, then words:

KEEP AWAY

Anders snorted. "Keep away? Keep away from what?"

But Kate felt afraid. As she held the lantern high, she saw more writing. Moving the lantern closer, she traced the words, letter by letter:

OR ELSE

"Or else what?" Anders scoffed.

"Keep away or else," read Kate, the fear within her growing. Suddenly she felt angry with Anders. "How can you laugh? Whoever wrote those words came through while we were in the barn. He came through *now*, during the day—"

"The night," Anders interrupted.

"But it's been dark only a short time. And in that time—"

"He came, wrote a message, and left," Anders finished for her.

"*If* he left," answered Kate. She looked over her shoulder to make sure no one stood behind her. Beyond the glow of the lantern, the shadows edged away into night.

Then the wind swept across the top of the bank, blowing new snow in her face. Kate stepped back. "Keep away from what?" she asked.

"From whatever we've been doing."

"I suppose." Kate thought about it for a moment. "Haven't been doing much, sitting in a house while it snowed. But this afternoon where did you go?"

"Across Rice Lake."

"And just before the blizzard, what did we do?"

It wasn't hard to remember. Kate answered her own question. "We found the milk can." Again she glanced over her shoulder. *"Keep away or else.* Or else *what*? What would he do?"

"What would he do?" her brother asked. "I can tell you."

In the light of the lantern Kate saw Anders grin.

"No, don't," she said quickly. "I don't think I want to hear."

"But you asked." His voice changed, sounding low and mysterious. "He'll creep up on you at night. As you walk from the house to the barn, he'll pounce on you!"

"Oh, *Anders!*" Kate clapped her hands over her ears. She refused to hear more. From now on she would dread the walk to the barn even more.

But she wasn't going to let Anders know. Not for anything would she let him know how she felt.

She returned to her pail of milk and picked it up. Flipping her braid over her shoulder, she walked to the farmhouse as though she didn't have a care in the world.

But when she reached the door, she saw the look in her brother's eyes. "After supper," she whispered. "We'll look for tracks after supper."

20

Snatched From the Fire

*F*or the first time in his life Anders helped Kate with supper dishes. Then they shrugged into their coats and went outside.

"Strange!" Anders said. "You're right. Whoever wrote that message had to come while we were in the barn."

Kate's fingers clenched with nervousness. "Maybe it's someone we know well."

"Someone we see every day without guessing he'd try to scare us," Anders said.

Holding out the lantern, Kate started across the yard. "When we were in the barn, I thought I heard something. But there weren't any sleigh bells."

Once again, whoever wrote the message seemed to have used a long pole. With the new covering of snow, it was easy to find the medium-sized boot prints Kate and Anders had seen before. Starting at the snowbank, they followed the prints along the plowed trail that passed the house.

Halfway to the barn, the boot prints suddenly vanished. Kate and Anders stood there, unable to believe what they were seeing.

"How can footsteps disappear in midair?" she asked.

"They can't," her brother answered. "But they have. See these prints beyond? They're entirely different."

Kate stared at them. "Different all right, but almost the same size!"

Holding the lantern close, Kate leaned down. "Look how the right boot turns, just slightly?" A step farther on, she pointed again. "And here the left boot twists a bit!"

Suddenly she laughed. "He stood there changing boots! See? From here on, a new set of prints!"

But in the next instant Kate's laughter died on her lips. "Who *is* this person? He knows we're watching him. He knows we'll try to follow." Tracking the man no longer seemed a game.

Anders took the farm lantern. "Just the same, let's see where his new boots take us."

Step by step they followed the prints to the water tank, then back to the trail. Near the tracks made by the runners of a sleigh, the boot prints vanished.

"Well, he's gone anyway." Kate felt relieved.

But Anders groaned. "We've lost him again! We're no better off than before. Worse, come to think of it."

"Worse?"

"We know how bold he is, coming into our yard again. We know how he plans, even bringing along an extra pair of boots. And he's doing everything he can to scare us off."

Kate shivered. "He's a dangerous man!" Then she remembered. "I didn't load wood in the tank heater." Earlier that winter she'd forgotten, and by morning the water turned into a block of ice.

Hurrying back to the water tank, she opened the lid of the stove. But the fire had gone out.

Kate groaned. Now she had to start all over again. Taking newspaper from the barn, she crumpled and lit it. As the flame caught, she lifted the stove lid.

In the light of the burning newspaper, Kate saw something. Reaching into the narrow pipe for loading wood, she pulled out a small piece of paper.

Then she felt heat on her hand. Quickly she dropped the burning newspaper in the snow.

"What're you doing?" asked Anders, clearly impatient.

As the newspaper turned into black flakes, then burned out, Kate spoke softly. "It's cold here. Let's go in the barn."

Once there she held the piece of white paper close to the lantern. The paper had caught in the pipe for loading wood.

The name of the person to whom the letter was addressed was charred and impossible to read. So, too, was the opening part of the letter. Kate read the remaining message aloud:

> *I opened your mail by accident. I found this check, made out to cash and sent by your old friend from New York. Are you still working with him to cheat people out of money? Are you being dishonest again? I had hoped your time in jail cured you of that weakness.*
>
> *I love you, my brother, but I plead with you. Send back the money while you can. Turn to honest work.*

Kate looked up. "It's signed 'Your sister,' and then the initial O."

Anders grinned. "This explains the missing checks from New York! The thief knows someone who writes the checks to him, instead of the Trade Lake Creamery. Whoever that person is sends the checks to the wrong address."

Kate thought about it. "With the slow mail service, it worked. That is, until his sister opened his mail."

"So all the thief has to do is go to his hometown and pick up his mail. If the checks from New York are made out to "cash," he can cash them anywhere. He'll get a lot more money than from the cream checks."

Slowly Kate folded the letter. "That's what I don't understand. When he'll get those big checks, why steal from the farmers? And why take the ledger?"

Anders shrugged. "I don't know. Maybe he's greedy. Or maybe he has a grudge, like Erik says. But I do know one thing. We have to go for help. Now. Tonight. Before he gets away."

Yet when they returned to the house, Mama was the one who needed help. "Will you stay with Lars for a bit?" she asked Kate. "He's sleeping, and I need to lie down. Anders, will you take care of Tina?"

Kate and Anders looked at each other. They both knew they couldn't leave.

In the bedroom Kate watched her younger brother sleep. She listened to his labored breathing.

Until recently, she'd paid little attention to Lars. Always she and Anders did things together. For the first time Kate wondered, *What was it like before I came? Has Lars been left out, because of me?*

He seldom complained about anything. Often Kate took him for granted, as though he were a younger copy of Anders. Lars's illness forced her to notice him as a person. She liked what she saw.

Now he lay limp, as though his body had no strength left. Beneath the freckles, his skin seemed flushed.

Kate reached over, felt his forehead. It was hot, too hot. Lars was burning up with fever.

A pang of fear shot through Kate—a fear so strong that she trembled. Even this morning, she could push fear to the back of her mind. No longer could she do that.

Will Lars die? The thought filled her with panic.

Going to the washstand, Kate dipped a cloth in cold water. Wringing it out, she placed it on Lars's forehead. Then she wet his face and arms with another cool cloth.

The nine-year-old stirred and opened eyes that were too bright. He seemed dazed, as though wondering where he was.

"Papa!" he cried out. "Papa, I see the horses!"

Kate leaned forward. "Papa isn't here right now."

Lars paid no attention. "Papa! I see the horses. See them down by the lake? They're thirsty. I'm thirsty too."

Hurrying out of the room, Kate called, "Mama!"

In the kitchen, Kate took the dipper and filled a glass with water from the covered pail. Returning to Lars, she held the glass to his lips. After one swallow he pushed it aside.

"Papa, I want to go swimming—"

His words became a mumble Kate couldn't understand. She looked up to see Mama at the door. Behind her stood Anders, and next to him, Tina.

"Papa, the water—" Lars's words were clear again. "It's so cool—"

"He's out of his head," said Mama. "He doesn't know what he's saying." She walked to the washstand and dipped another cloth in the water.

Lars's eyes glazed with fever. As he looked up into Kate's face, his vision seemed to clear.

"Kate?" he asked, his voice weak. "Kate, are you scared?"

"Scared, Lars? What do you mean?"

"Don't be scared, Kate. You don't have to be scared. The angels are all around us."

Quick tears flooded Kate's eyes. *Is he dying?* she wondered. Her knees felt weak, as though they would no longer hold her up.

Then Anders stood beside her. For the second time in two days he took Kate's hand. He seemed to sense she needed it. With his free hand he reached out to his brother.

"Lars," Anders said, his voice gruff. "You're right. We can't see the angels the way you do. But they *are* all around us."

Blinking away the tears in her eyes, Kate looked up at Anders. Somehow he always surprised her.

"Jesus is here too," said Mama, coming to stand on Kate's other side. "Jesus loves you, Lars."

"I know." His voice was weak.

"And we love you." Mama and Kate spoke almost together.

"I know." Lars's voice was weaker yet. He closed his eyes and lay still, his face pale against the pillowcase.

Kate barely breathed. "Is he—"

Mama shook her head. "No." She led them into the kitchen. "You must go for Dr. Jonas."

Kate's heart pounded against her chest. The doctor lived miles away, beyond the village of Trade Lake.

"Tell him it's an emergency," urged Mama. "That Lars is very sick. I hope we're not too late."

Anders met Mama's eyes, but Kate saw her suffering and looked away.

Anders scribbled on a piece of paper. Tucking the message inside the small bag Kate had made, he fastened it to a rope.

Hurrying to the door, he shouted. When Lutfisk came, Anders tied the rope around the dog's neck.

Opening the door again, Anders went out on the step. "Go get Erik!" he said.

Lutfisk barked.

Anders pointed across the field. "Erik!" he commanded.

With another bark, the dog streaked away into the night.

21

Ride Into Fear

*K*ate's fingers fumbled with haste as she pulled on her warmest clothing. When she and Anders were ready to leave, Mama put one hand on Kate's shoulder, the other on Anders's. "God will go with you," she said.

As Anders and Kate hurried outside, she saw the thermometer. "Almost forty below," she told Anders. "It'll be even worse by morning."

In the barn they worked together to harness Wildfire.

"What did you tell Erik?" Kate asked.

"To meet us at the fork in the trail." Anders moved toward the door. "I'll get the cutter."

When Kate brought Wildfire outside, Anders backed the mare between the shafts of the small sleigh. Kate put in heavy blankets, then wrapped her long scarf around her face.

As they settled themselves in the cutter, Anders called out, "Giddyup!" Wildfire pranced across the yard, her black tail swishing. At the bottom of the steep hill, her long legs reached out. She seemed to sense their need to hurry.

When they came to the fork in the trail, Erik jumped into the cutter. Lutfisk was with him and bounded alongside.

"What's wrong?" Erik asked.

"Lars is really sick," said Kate. She felt like crying just talking about it. "We have to go for the doctor."

"What happened?"

"His temperature shot up. He was talking strange—out of his head. Mama's says it's an emergency."

Soon they crossed Rice Lake. As they turned south toward the village of Trade Lake, they found the road packed into a smooth trail. The moon edged above the horizon, orange and round.

Inside her wool mittens Kate wiggled her fingers. Already they tingled with cold. She thrust her hands beneath the heavy blanket.

Fear settled like a knot deep inside. "What if Lars dies?" she asked.

The question hung between them, seeming even colder than the January air. Then Anders flicked the reins and urged Wildfire on. "It'd be pretty awful."

Under the full moon Kate saw the scarf had slipped from her brother's face. A tear shone on his cheek.

It startled Kate. She remembered only once when she'd seen tears in her brother's eyes. Then he'd been badly hurt. Even in these last days with Papa out in the storm, Anders seldom spoke about his worry.

Now he pulled the scarf across his face. Kate wondered if he was trying to hide his feelings.

The creamery was dark when they passed through the center of town. As they crossed Trade River, the mare's hooves thundered on the wooden bridge.

"I sure hope Doc is home," said Anders.

Neither Erik nor Kate answered. For many miles around there was no one else who could help.

When they reached the doctor's house, a kerosene lamp glowed through the window. Throwing the reins into Kate's lap, Anders jumped down. Erik ran for the stable. By the time Doc Jonas hurried out with his black bag, Erik had the horse ready.

With a wave of the hand, the doctor flung himself into the saddle. Digging in his heels, he broke into a gallop.

Anders followed at a slower pace with Wildfire and the cutter.

"Will Doc Jonas get there in time?" Kate asked.

"I don't know." Anders spoke so low that Kate could barely hear. "But we've done our best."

As they passed back through the village of Trade Lake, Wildfire slowed down, as if by habit. Just then Kate caught a faint glow through a creamery window.

"Stop," she said to Anders, close to his ear. "There's someone there."

"I can't stop here," Anders whispered back. "By now he's heard Wildfire."

Rounding the corner by the creamery, they started up the hill. A safe distance away, Anders pulled Wildfire to a halt. Jumping out, he tied the mare's lead rope to a tree.

The three crept back to the creamery. At the window where they'd seen the light, they peered in. The small glow of a flickering candle broke the darkness.

A man wearing a red and black mackinaw leaned over the buttermaker's desk. As he looked through papers, he held each one to the light.

"Who is it?" Kate whispered. With his back turned to them and a cap covering his hair, it was impossible to tell.

Anders shushed Kate and motioned to her and Erik. Careful to walk in soft snow that left no sound, the three edged back from the window.

When far enough away not to be heard, Kate spoke again. "Who is it? Mr. Grimm or Mr. Fenton? From the back they both look the same."

Erik shook his head, and Anders shrugged. "We have to go for help," he said.

Together they agreed that they needed more than one grown-up.

"I'll tell Mr. Bloomquist," Kate said. She knew where he lived.

"He left today for the buttermaker's convention," Erik told her. "At least he was supposed to."

"I'll go for Andrew Anderson," said Anders.

In that moment Kate remembered what Big Gust told them. "Let's ask Reverend Pickle too."

"You get him, Kate," Anders said. "Take Wildfire. You've got the farthest to go."

Kate's stomach tightened. She hadn't handled Wildfire since before Christmas, and then only a few times. Could she remember how?

But Anders took it for granted that she would. Quickly he gave directions to Reverend Pickle's house.

"I'll stay here," said Erik. "If the man leaves before you get back, I'll follow him." Quietly he edged away, back toward the creamery.

Anders and Kate hurried to the cutter. "Remember what you do?" he asked.

Kate nodded. Often she'd watched Anders. Just the same, she wondered if she could manage the spirited horse.

"Don't slow down when you pass the creamery," Anders warned. "Keep going as if you don't see anything." Then he, too, slipped off into the night, heading north to Andrew Anderson's farm.

Kate called "Giddyup!" and Wildfire turned her head, as though hearing Kate's uncertainty. Just the same, the mare obeyed. At the top of Mission Hill Kate turned around, directing Wildfire south, back over the way they'd come.

As she neared the creamery, she saw Erik crouched outside a window. Like a shadow he edged away, dark along the wall.

Kate glanced toward the window. The candle still burned. The man was nowhere in sight.

Where is he? thought Kate. *Did he hear Wildfire coming? Or did he see Erik?* If the man went out a back door, he could creep around the building, catching the boy.

I should warn Erik, Kate told herself and slowed the mare.

Then she remembered her brother's words. "Keep going. Don't stop at the creamery."

Kate flicked the reins. Wildfire's hooves pounded across the bridge.

The full moon rode high, lighting the snow as if it were day. Reverend Pickle's farm bordered on two lakes. "You'll know it," Anders said. "There's an artesian well in his front yard."

An artesian well? Kate knew such a well was one where water

flowed to the surface under its own pressure. But how would it look? She should have asked Anders.

In the next moment Kate forgot her question. As she passed into the woods, the trees cast long shadows.

Kate slid to the center of the seat, as far from the trees as possible. Yet the branches reached out, dark and threatening.

At Four Corners, she turned Wildfire. Here in an area with fewer trees, drifts were again filling the packed-down road. As Wildfire lunged into them, snow sprayed up. More than once the mare slowed her pace, fighting her way through.

Soon the way again led between trees. As Kate turned the mare onto another road, the woods seemed alive. Like pointing fingers, long pine branches reached out. Then an owl screeched, shattering the night air.

Kate trembled. "I can't do it!" she cried out to the darkness. "I'm going back!" The wind caught her words and flung them into her face.

She reined in Wildfire, then remembered Lars. Had the doctor reached him by now? Was Lars still fighting for life?

And where was Papa? Somewhere in this awful cold, struggling through drifts to reach home?

And her brother Anders? *Scaredy-cat, he calls me!* Usually Kate feared small, imaginary things. Now she faced something real. No doubt the thief would leave the area tonight.

Fighting down panic, Kate clucked to Wildfire, urging her on. A short distance away, she saw a farm with what must be an artesian well. In spite of the cold, water gushed from a pipe, spilling down a slope to create a pathway of ice.

I was so close, thought Kate. *What if I had turned back?*

Leaving Wildfire at a rail, she hurried up the steps and pounded on the door. A moment later a woman with gray hair invited Kate inside.

"Mrs. Pickle?" she asked. "Is Reverend Pickle here? We need his help."

"I'm sorry," the woman answered. "He was called out an hour ago. Is there something I can do?"

Unable to believe such bad news, Kate stared at her. "I came so far. He's really not here?"

Just then a heavyset man passed through the hallway behind the woman. The man wore a red and black mackinaw.

Without thinking, Kate fled from the house. Leaping into the cutter, she flicked the reins across Wildfire's back. The mare headed back over the same road.

When Kate came to her senses, she pulled off a mitten. Quickly she felt her scarf to be sure her ears, nose, and cheeks were covered. If not, they would soon be too numb for her to know. Within a minute she'd suffer frostbite.

Gazing through the narrow slits for her eyes, Kate directed Wildfire. Soon she let the mare find her way home. That way led where Kate wanted to go—through the village of Trade Lake.

Once again trees closed around her, and her fear returned. Who was the man in the hallway? Gunnar Grimm? Too late she remembered him saying that he stayed with Reverend Pickle.

Was he also the man who entered Josie's house? And the man who looked through papers at the creamery? If he slipped out while they talked, he could have reached Pickle's farm before Kate.

Where was that man now? Somewhere behind, coming after her, trying to catch up?

"I'm all alone on this cold dark road," Kate muttered. From behind any tree someone could step out and leap into the cutter.

Kate shivered with fear. Before long, that shivering changed into a trembling that would not stop. But then she felt ashamed. *What am I doing, feeling sorry for myself when Lars might be dying?*

"God will go with you," Mama had said. Her words seemed an echo of Papa's letter.

"Fear thou not, for I am with thee," Kate told herself now, repeating God's promise. "Be not dismayed; for I am thy God."

Over and over she said the words, clinging to them like life itself. "I will strengthen thee; yea, I will help thee."

In that moment God's promise became more real than ever before. Kate felt sure of something. *No matter what happens, God is with me!*

The trees still reached out to clutch her. The road still seemed dark and lonely. But deep inside, Kate felt peaceful, unafraid.

When she reached the village of Trade Lake, she saw no light in the creamery. Nor was there light in any of the houses. Tightening the reins, she stopped Wildfire to give herself time to think.

Since leaving Erik and Anders, Kate had taken it for granted she'd find them again at the creamery. Yet no shadow emerged from between the buildings. Either one of the boys would have stepped out.

What do I do now? Kate wondered.

In that instant a question came to her mind. Where would the thief go when he left the creamery?

Only a desperate man would be out on a night like this. In such bitter cold, people stayed inside. That left the thief free to do whatever he wanted. If he planned to leave the area, he'd go to Rice Lake for the milk can. Erik would follow.

"Giddyup!" said Kate, and Wildfire moved out.

At the southwest corner of Rice Lake, Wildfire left the road, crossed the field, and entered the woods. Partway through the trees, she stopped.

Kate urged Wildfire on, but the mare tossed her head and would not move. "Oh, Anders," Kate grumbled. "You shouldn't have let me take this horse."

She flicked the reins, and the mare took one step forward, then another. Once more she stopped.

"Go ahead, Wildfire," said Kate, trying to sound as though she were boss.

The mare's ears turned to the sound of Kate's voice. Yet the horse would not move.

Climbing down from the cutter, Kate walked forward to take the bridle. In that moment she saw what the mare sensed. Shadows. Shadows moving among the trees.

Kate's heart pounded. Her fingers knotted in fear. Who was it? What was there?

Wildfire lifted her head as though to whinny. Quickly Kate reached up, touched the mare's muzzle and quieted her. When Wildfire stood still, Kate took the bells from the harness, muffling the sound.

"It's all right, girl," she whispered, wishing she could believe her own words. Moving back to the cutter, she pushed the bells under the blanket where they wouldn't jingle.

Returning to the mare, Kate grabbed hold of the bridle. Together they took one step forward, then another.

Off to the right a shadow moved. Kate froze. Who was it? Friend or enemy?

As she stood there, the shadow blended with the trunk of a tree. Like an enemy breathing on the back of her neck, fear again gripped Kate. She tried to push it aside, but couldn't.

Then there was something she knew, *Maybe what counts is doing the right thing, no matter how scared I am.*

Ahead lay Rice Lake and beyond that, Windy Hill Farm. Should she wait or go on?

As she felt the cold, Kate knew she had no choice. If she didn't keep moving, she'd die, standing there in the sub-zero cold.

Slowly she lifted one foot, then another, forcing herself ahead. "Fear thou not, for I am with thee." She repeated the words to herself. Drawing a deep breath, she took a third step.

Suddenly, from out of the darkness, someone stood behind her. Startled, Kate jumped. In the next instant, she felt a hand over her mouth, cutting off her cry.

22

Bone-Chilling Surprises

$\mathcal{G}$asping, Kate struggled to free herself. The strong arm held her prisoner.

"Sorry, Kate," said a low voice.

She tried to swing around, but the person would not let her move. "Shhh!" he warned, again speaking softly.

In that instant Kate knew it was Erik. As she sagged with relief, he let her go.

"What do you mean, scaring me like that?" she asked in an angry whisper.

"Be quiet!" he warned again. "The thief is ahead. He built a fire on the ice."

Then Kate saw the flames. Even through the trees and bushes the light shone for some distance.

Taking Wildfire's bridle, Erik led the mare off the path to a sheltered spot. Tying her lead rope to a tree, he threw a horse blanket over her back.

"Where's Anders?" Kate whispered when Erik returned.

He pointed ahead. A short distance off to the right, a shadow left a tree, raised a hand, then stepped back close to the trunk.

"I couldn't get Reverend Pickle," she said.

Erik leaned close. "Andrew Anderson is here. I hope we're

enough." Again he pointed, this time off to the left.

At first Kate couldn't spot Mr. Anderson. Then with the help of the full moon, she saw a tree trunk that looked thicker at the bottom than it should.

Together Kate and Erik crept forward. Close to the shoreline they knelt down behind a bush and peered through its leafless branches. In front of them clumps of bent-over grass marked the boggy end of the lake. There was only one safe place to cross—the trail Anders and Erik had packed down.

From this distance the fire seemed small. Beyond the dancing flames, the branches of the tall oak reached upward.

Then, in the light of the fire, Kate saw a heavyset man in a black and red mackinaw. Holding out his mittened hands, the man warmed himself by the fire. Then he picked up an ice chisel and started chopping.

Kate breathed deep. No wonder Anders and Erik and Mr. Anderson waited, watching from the cover of trees.

In the bitter air, minutes seemed like hours as the man chopped a hole. Twice he stopped to warm himself, then returned to his work. Whenever he turned his back, Kate and Erik stamped their feet, trying to keep from freezing.

Finally the man knelt down next to the hole. Reaching into the water, he pulled out the milk can and set it on the ice. Just as quickly, he pulled off his wet gloves and replaced them with dry ones.

From this distance it looked as if a rope now held the stone, instead of a chain. Taking a tool from his pocket, the man cut the stone free and dropped it back into the water. Shouldering the milk can, he picked up his chisel and started toward them.

Andrew Anderson moved onto the path, then the lake. Anders and Erik followed, and with them, Kate. As they drew close to the man, Kate saw his sandy colored mustache and beard. LeRoy Fenton!

For one instant surprise and fear flickered across his face. Then a mask slid down. "Hello!" he said smoothly, as he came close. "Fancy seeing you here!"

In that moment Kate spotted something. On the underside of the man's raised arm, a tear in his mackinaw.

Mr. Anderson stepped in front of him. "Just a minute. I have some questions for you."

"Certainly, certainly. Be glad to talk to you any time. But not in this cold. How about tomorrow at the creamery?"

"I want to talk now," said Mr. Anderson.

Instead, LeRoy Fenton started around the older man. Erik and Anders moved quickly. But just then a dark shape appeared on the path, running toward them. When the shape barked, Kate knew it was Lutfisk.

Within three feet of Fenton, the dog stopped and growled deep in his throat.

Mr. Fenton stepped sideways, but Lutfisk moved with him, baring his teeth.

The milk can still on his shoulder, LeRoy Fenton stopped. "Whose dog is this?" he asked, sounding less smooth than usual.

"He's mine," said Anders with pride in his voice.

"Well, call him off," he ordered.

"After you've talked to Mr. Anderson," Anders replied.

In that moment Fenton lifted his head, seeming to listen. Along the trail, boots squeaked on the packed snow. The steps moved closer, closer.

A minute later someone stepped onto the ice. A man in a black and red mackinaw. Kate's heart pounded. Gunnar Grimm! Was she right in believing he was innocent? Or were the two men partners?

Kate glanced at Mr. Anderson. He, too, stood waiting, watching.

Mr. Grimm faced LeRoy Fenton. "Mighty cold night to try leaving town."

The mask on Fenton's face seemed to crack, then break with anger. "What is this, an ice party?"

Mr. Grimm chuckled. "Nope! It's time for explanations. Why don't you tell them how you took the cream checks and ledger?"

"And how you had the New York checks sent to your hometown!" said Anders.

The milk can still on his shoulder, LeRoy Fenton turned to Mr. Anderson. "You know I'm trustworthy. Don't believe a word they say."

"But I do," answered Mr. Anderson.

Suddenly Fenton threw the ice chisel toward the dog. Backing away, he broke into a run. For one instant he glanced toward the wheat-colored grass, then veered from the boggy area. Changing direction, he headed for the southeastern shore.

Lutfisk started after him.

"Stay, Lutfisk!" Anders called.

The dog stopped and looked back, clearly not wanting to obey.

"Stay!" commanded Anders again. Lutfisk sat down on the ice and woofed.

"Stop, Fenton!" shouted Mr. Anderson. Across the end of the lake, the snow stretched out, clean and unbroken under the full moon.

As the distance widened between them, Kate felt sick. "He'll get away!"

"No, he won't," said Erik.

Then she remembered. The spring holes!

Again Mr. Anderson shouted. "Fenton! Stop! Don't go any farther!"

One hand still supporting the milk can, Mr. Fenton looked back. The next instant he wavered. The snow gave way, and the can fell from his shoulder.

"Help!" he cried as he slipped through the ice. His arms flailed in the cold water.

The others started toward him. Using the ice chisel, Anders tested each step before taking it. Erik and the men followed in his footprints.

"Get a blanket, Kate," said Erik. "But watch where you walk." Hurrying to the cutter, Kate pulled out a heavy blanket. By the time she returned, the men had Fenton out of the water and into clothing loaned by the others.

As LeRoy Fenton stood by the fire, he shook with cold. Mr. Anderson put the blanket around his shoulders.

"Are you a detective?" Kate asked Mr. Grimm when she joined them around the fire. "From New York, I bet."

When Mr. Grimm smiled, Kate remembered thinking he wasn't the grouch he seemed.

"I was trying to solve a robbery in New York," he said. "All my leads pointed here. But I didn't know who the man was. You're the one who tipped me off."

"Me?" asked Kate. "How?"

"By being curious. You asked, 'How come everyone harvesting ice is new at it?' I've been watching Fenton ever since. Tonight I followed your cutter tracks here."

As the men started to lead LeRoy Fenton away, Kate faced him with a question. "Why did you put salt in the butter?"

"I'm a better buttermaker!" he said. "The job should have gone to me!" Then his mouth snapped shut, as though realizing he'd given himself away.

Standing at the fire with Anders and Erik, Kate spoke softly. "Mr. Fenton's the real grouch, not Mr. Grimm."

"Can you imagine?" Erik said. "Making all that trouble because of a grudge? What a way to get even!"

"Maybe he thought he'd still get the job," Anders said as he went for Wildfire.

When the brothers returned, Kate climbed into the cutter. "The farmers will get paid!" she exclaimed.

"And the creamery will get its checks from New York," Erik said. He started to laugh. "Curious Kate! It doesn't take a detective to figure that out!"

Anders laughed, too, and Mr. Grimm's words seemed funny even to Kate. But now that the excitement was over, she could think of only one thing. "I wonder what's happened to Lars."

When they reached Windy Hill Farm, Erik told Anders, "I'll put Wildfire in the barn."

When Kate and Anders entered the kitchen, it was quiet. *Too* quiet, Kate thought.

A tall bearded man stood by the cookstove. Was it the doctor?

The man turned. His lips were cracked, his skin reddened by wind and cold. The heavily bearded man seemed a stranger.

Then Kate cried, "Papa!"

He opened his arms, and she walked into them. She felt his bear hug, then heard the emotion in his voice. "Kate! My newest daughter!"

When she stood back, she saw the relief in Anders's face. He tried to speak, but no words came. When he reached out to shake his father's hand, Papa put his arms around him.

Then Mama stood at the door to the dining room.

"Lars?" Kate and Anders asked together.

"He's better," Mama answered softly, her eyes as blue as the new dress she wore. "The doctor says Lars passed the crisis. He'll be all right."

Throwing off their coats, Kate and Anders tiptoed into the bedroom.

Lars lay with his eyes closed, his face pale against the pillow. His red hair was matted, twisted every which way, but his skin no longer seemed flushed with fever.

As they stood there, Lars opened his eyes. A slight smile came to his lips. Then he drifted back to sleep.

Swallowing around the lump in her throat, Kate looked at Anders.

One tear slid down his cheek, then another. When he saw Kate watching, he brushed the tears away, but did not seem ashamed.

Returning to the kitchen, Kate and Anders found Erik there. As they gathered near the warmth of the cookstove, Papa put his arm around Mama's shoulders.

Kate's heart leaped. "You're really home!" she said to Papa. "Now spring will come!"

Anders grinned. "With maple syrup—and logs floating down the rivers."

"And another mystery, I suppose." Erik winked at Kate.

"Maybe we'll find out what happened to Mama's brother," Kate said, then wished she hadn't spoken.

But tonight not even the thought of Ben could destroy Mama's happiness. In the lamplight a golden curl dropped over her forehead. She slipped a hand inside Papa's, and her lips curved in a smile.

As the heat of the stove reached Kate's fingers, another warmth crept into her heart. She looked around, needing to see those she loved. Mama, Papa, Anders. And upstairs in bed, Tina. In the next room, Lars. *My family!* thought Kate.

Then Erik moved closer to the stove. Kate saw the relief in

his eyes. She had another person she could trust. *My special friend!*

Within the warmth of that circle, spring had already entered the room.

Acknowledgments

"Aw, come on now!" you might be thinking if you live in a warm and sunny climate. "Thirty-three and forty degrees below zero?"

Yes, that's right. Now and then—not often, of course—even those of us who live in northwest Wisconsin complain about the weather. Other times we feel almost proud to be survivors. And so, I assure you, the temperatures given in this book were actually recorded in a 1907 issue of the newspaper, *Journal of Burnett County*.

In spite of the hazards or because of them, those who live in this area are a warm and helpful people. I offer my heartfelt thanks to those who described the early Trade Lake area for me: Imogene Erickson, Emma Bergstrom Haight, Robert and Jean Hinrichs, Clare and Dorothy Melin, and Pharis and Kathryn Stower.

Others gave needed information or special help at just the right time: Robert Anderson, Alice and Leon Biederman, Diane Brask, Wade Brask, Alwin and Imogene Christopherson, Betty Coleman, Maurice and Arleth Erickson, Alton Jensen, Dick and Lois Klawitter, Randy and Renee Klawitter, Henry Peterson, Elaine Roub, Helen Tyberg, and my parents, Alvar and Lydia Walfrid.

Walter and Ella Johnson offered unique wisdom in a variety

of ways, including the fine art of bartering, how to harvest and store ice, and the mysterious uses of milk cans and butter tubs.

Mildred Hedlund helped me with Big Gust, as did Eunice Kanne and her book, *Big Gust: Grantsburg's Legendary Giant*. I'm also grateful to J. C. Ryan for his book, *Early Loggers in Minnesota*, the Grantsburg Historical Society, and all the librarians at the Grantsburg Public Library.

Dale Olson, world champion cheesemaker for the Burnett County Dairy, Alpha, Wisconsin, helped me begin my search for information about creameries. A father and son team, John D. Wuethrich and Dallas Wuethrich, of the John Wuethrich Creamery at Greenwood, Wisconsin, showed me the contrast between buttermaking in the early part of the century and the automated, up-to-date methods now used.

Once again, my husband Roy offered ideas, encouragement, and love. Jerry Foley, Penelope Stokes, and Terry White gave suggestions for the manuscript. Charette Barta, Doris Holmlund, Ron Klug, and the entire Bethany team gave valuable editorial assistance.

Finally, I want to give my thanks to you, the readers of this series. Sometimes you read these books by yourself, tucked away in a quiet spot. Other times you read aloud as a family, a community group or classroom. Whichever way you follow Kate and Anders in the Adventures of the Northwoods, you encourage me by saying, "I've read all of 'em. When's the next book coming out?"